MEET THE FORTUNES!

Fortune of the Month: Callum Fortune

Age: 30

Vital Statistics: Tall and lean, charismatic, gold-flecked deep brown eyes and a kiss-worthy tan. As Becky Averill describes him—a Greek god come to life...or as close as one is likely to get in Rambling Rose, Texas.

Claim to Fame: Callum made his money in real estate. But he's not one of "those" Fortunes. His family is from Florida, and Callum's father has warned him and his seven (!) siblings to avoid their Texas relations at all costs.

Romantic Prospects: Some would say Callum is married to his job. That's as close to marriage as he wants to get. He's not going to make *that* mistake a second time.

"I'm not in Rambling Rose to stay. As soon as my projects are completed, I'll be on the road to my next adventure. So I need to keep things simple.

"There's nothing simple about Becky. She's beautiful, sure, but everything about her screams commitment—from her cozy home to her supercute toddler twins. I should cut and run before it's too late. Before I leave three lovely ladies in the lurch. Before I feel tempted to stick around and become the family man I know I can't be..."

Dear Reader,

Happy New Year! It's a thrill to be starting 2020 with a new Fortunes of Texas series. These characters have become so familiar to me, and the authors and readers who love them feel like an extended family in the best way possible.

I love a man who's good with children, so Callum Fortune is such an appealing hero. Especially because he's adorably clueless to the fact that he's meant to be a family man. But when he meets Becky Averill and her cute twin toddlers, he can't resist. As a single mom, Becky has her hands full, but somehow Callum manages to find a place in her busy life and her heart. Neither of them expects to discover love in the small town of Rambling Rose, Texas. But if they find the courage to follow their hearts, it could bring them the kind of happiness they've only imagined.

I hope you enjoy joining Callum and Becky on their journey to happily-ever-after and meeting some of the newest additions to the Fortune family.

Please stop by if you have a chance at michellemajor.com. And look for my new miniseries, Welcome to Starlight, coming in March from Harlequin Special Edition.

Happy reading!

Michelle

Fortune's Fresh Start

—

Michelle Major

⬡ HARLEQUIN®SPECIAL EDITION

Special thanks and acknowledgment are given to Michelle Major for her contribution to The Fortunes of Texas: Rambling Rose continuity.

Recycling programs
for this product may
not exist in your area.

ISBN-13: 978-1-335-89428-1
ISBN 13: 978-1-335-08104-9 (DTC Edition)

Fortune's Fresh Start

Copyright © 2019 by Harlequin Books S.A.

www.Harlequin.com

Printed in U.S.A.

Michelle Major grew up in Ohio but dreamed of living in the mountains. Soon after graduating with a degree in journalism, she pointed her car west and settled in Colorado. Her life and house are filled with one great husband, two beautiful kids, a few furry pets and several well-behaved reptiles. She's grateful to have found her passion writing stories with happy endings. Michelle loves to hear from her readers at michellemajor.com.

To Jennie. Thanks for all the fun times and morning chats. I treasure our friendship.

Chapter One

"You're going to be late to your own party."

Callum Fortune turned at the sound of his sister's teasing voice. "It's a ribbon-cutting ceremony, Squeak. Not a cocktail gala."

Stephanie Fortune, younger than Callum by three years but the oldest of David and Marci Fortune's four daughters, approached Callum's shiny silver truck. Her pale red hair was pulled back in a braid and she wore dark jeans and a gray sweater that could have benefited from a lint roller. As a vet tech and all-around animal lover, Stephanie was often covered in dog and cat fur. Or whatever breed of animal she was caring for that day. Her heart was as big as her personality and one of the things Callum loved most about her.

"It's past time you stop calling me that," she told him with an exaggerated eye roll. "What if someone in Rambling Rose hears you and the nickname catches on? I'd be mortified."

"It's our secret," he promised with a wink. "But you'll always be my Pipsqueak no matter where life takes either of us."

"I'm home," Stephanie said, her tone definitive. "There's no other place I'd rather be."

"Then I'm glad you came along on this adventure."

Callum agreed there was something special about Rambling Rose, Texas. The small town sat equidistant between the larger metropolitan areas of Houston and Austin. Callum had first learned about it through a documentary, *The Faded Rose*, he'd watched late one night when he'd had trouble sleeping. Shortly after, he'd traveled to Paseo, Texas, with his father for the wedding of David's brother, Gerald Robinson—or Jerome Fortune as he was once known. On a whim, Callum had driven to Rambling Rose and within a week he'd made offers on a ranch in a gated community outside town as well as a half-dozen commercial properties.

Real estate development was Callum's passion, and he'd made a name for himself in his home state of Florida and a good portion of the Southeast as someone who could revitalize small-town communities by working together with residents, local businesses and government agencies. He loved the challenge of breathing new life into spaces that had seen better days.

From that perspective, Rambling Rose was a perfect next step in Callum's career. The town had a long history in Texas but was sorely in need of a face-lift and someone to invest in the local economy. Callum's father, David, had his doubts. The entire Fortune family, both new and established members, had been shaken by the kidnapping that had almost ruined Gerald's wedding to his first love, Deborah, six months ago. David was a huge success in his own right thanks to his wildly profitable video game empire and had reservations about claiming his place in the extended Fortune brood even before that shocking turn of events. Even though the day had turned out happily in the end, David's protective instincts had kicked into high gear. He'd encouraged his eight children to stay far removed from any sort of involvement with the Texas Fortunes.

He and Marci, Callum's beloved stepmother, had been understandably concerned at Callum's rash decision to move to the small town, especially when his older stepbrother, Steven, younger brother, Dillon, and half sister, Stephanie, came with him. But Callum trusted his instincts when it came to real estate. He had no doubt Rambling Rose was the right decision, and his siblings' joining him was an added bonus.

He stood with Stephanie in the parking lot of the new Rambling Rose Pediatric Center, which was due to officially open its doors in two days. Callum was proud of everything his crew and the subcontractors he'd hired had accomplished in the past few months.

The building, which was situated about ten minutes north of Rambling Rose's quaint downtown area, had been almost completely gutted and rebuilt to house a state-of-the-art health facility where local children would receive primary medical, dental and behavioral health care at a facility designed just for them.

"We should go in," he said before Stephanie asked the inevitable question of whether he saw himself staying in Rambling Rose long-term. She wouldn't have wanted to hear his answer, but the thought of committing to the town longer than it would take to finish their projects made his skin itch.

Since he'd started his construction company, his modus operandi had always been to go with the work. He focused his efforts on small-town revitalizations but once he'd met his goals in a community, Callum moved on.

He wasn't a forever type of guy, at least not anymore.

"How are things at the vet clinic?" Stephanie asked as she fell into step next to him.

"On schedule to open next month," he answered, giving her a gentle nudge. "Don't worry, Squeak. We'll make sure you're still gainfully employed."

She gave him a playful nudge. "What do I have to do to get you to stop calling me that?"

"The dishes and my laundry for a week."

"Done."

He chuckled. "I should have held out for a month."

"Don't push your luck. I know how much you hate folding clothes."

"Been there, done that," he told her. He'd been three and his brother Dillon two when their father had married Marci. She'd had two boys of her own that she brought to the marriage: Steven, who was two years older than Callum, and Wiley, who was Callum's age. They'd had Stephanie right away and the triplets had followed five years after that. Marci was a great mother and treated all the kids with the same love and kindness. But the pregnancies had taken a toll on her health.

As a young boy, Callum had found himself responsible for the girls and running much of the household while his father focused on the explosive success of his first video game launch. The role had come naturally to Callum, but the added responsibility had robbed him of much of his childhood. He'd managed laundry for a household of ten from the time he was in elementary school until Marci's health had improved.

He didn't regret the time he'd dedicated to his siblings, but it definitely made him less inclined to take on more domestic tasks than were necessary to function as an adult.

"You still can't fold a fitted sheet the right way," Stephanie said in the flippant tone she'd perfected as an adorable but annoying little sister.

"No one can," he countered.

"Martha Stewart has a tutorial on it."

He shook his head as they approached the entrance of the pediatric center, where a small crowd had gathered. "I'm not watching Martha Stewart."

A flash of color caught his eye, and he noticed a woman pushing a double stroller toward the entrance. Two toddlers sat in the side-by-side seats, and one girl's blanket had slipped off her lap. The corner of the fabric was tangled in the wheel and the girls' frazzled-looking mother struggled to free it.

"There are Mom and Dad, with Steven and Dillon," Stephanie told him, taking a step toward their family, who stood near the swath of ceremonial ribbon that stretched in front of the center's entrance.

"Be there in a sec."

Without waiting for an answer, Callum jogged toward the woman and her two charges.

"Can I help?" he asked, offering a smile to the toddlers, who were mirror images of each other. Twins. No wonder their mom seemed stressed. He remembered what a handful his triplet sisters had been at that age.

The woman, who knelt on the pavement in a bright

blue dress, looked up at him. Callum promptly forgot his own name.

She was beyond beautiful…at least to him.

A lock of whiskey-hued hair fell across her cheek, and she tucked it behind her ear with a careless motion. Her features were conventional by most standards—a heart-shaped face, large brown eyes with thick lashes and creamy skin that turned an enchanting shade of pink as she met his gaze. Her mouth was full and her nose pert, but somehow everything came together to make her stunning. The sparkle in her gaze and the way her lips parted just a bit had him feeling like he'd been knocked in the head.

"It's caught in the wheel," she said, and it took him a moment to snap back to reality.

"Mama," one of the girls whined, tugging on the other end of the blanket.

"We'll get your blankie, Luna." The woman patted her daughter's leg. "This nice man is going to help."

Nice man. Callum wasn't sure he'd ever heard anyone describe him as "nice" but he'd take the compliment. He tried to remember the definition of the word while forcing himself to ignore the spark of attraction to a stranger who was probably some equally nice man's wife.

He crouched down next to the twins' mom and carefully extricated the fabric from the spokes of the wheel. It took only a minute and he heard an audible sigh of relief next to him once the blanket was free.

"Bankie," the girl shouted as she tugged the pink-and-yellow-checked blanket into her lap.

"Mama," her sister yelled like she wanted to be in on the action and then popped a pacifier into her mouth.

"Thank you," the woman said as they both straightened.

Callum was about to introduce himself when she stumbled a step. Without thinking, he reached out a hand to steady her.

"Are you okay?"

She flashed a sheepish smile. "Sorry. I stood up too fast. I didn't have time for breakfast today but managed two cups of coffee. Low blood sugar."

Callum had to bite back an invitation to go get breakfast with him even as he surreptitiously glanced at her left hand. No wedding ring, which didn't necessarily mean anything. Still, he could—

"Callum!"

He turned at the sound of his name. Steven waved at him from across the clusters of people gathered for the ceremony. Right. He was here for business, not to lose his head over a pretty woman.

His turn for an apologetic smile. "I have to go," he said.

She nodded. "Thanks again."

"You should eat something," he told her, then forced himself to wave at the girls and turn away after his brother called to him again.

Odd how difficult it was to walk away from a perfect stranger.

"The pediatric center would just be a dream for this community without the work of Callum, Steven and Dillon Fortune and everyone at Fortune Brothers Construction."

Becky Averill watched as Rambling Rose's effervescent mayor, Ellie Hernandez, motioned for the brothers to join her in front of the blue ribbon. How was it possible that Becky's stroller catastrophe hero was also the man she had to thank for her new job?

When the pediatric center officially opened a few days from now, she'd be the head nurse in the primary care department, reporting directly to Dr. Parker Green, who was heading up the entire center.

It was such a huge step up from her last position working part-time for an older family practice doctor who saw patients only a few days a week. In fact, it was Becky's dream job, one that would provide a livable wage, great health benefits for her and her girls as well as on-site day care. She couldn't believe how far she'd come from that horrible moment two years ago when a police officer had knocked on her door to relay the news that her husband had died in a car accident.

Becky had been only nine weeks pregnant when Rick died. They hadn't even learned she was expecting twins yet. Everything about her pregnancy had become a blur after that, as if she'd been living in some kind of hazy fog that never lifted.

Of course, things had become crystal clear the moment she heard her baby's first cry. Luna had been born two minutes before Sasha, but both babies filled Becky's heart with a new kind of hope for a future.

Her parents had wanted her to move back to the suburbs of Houston, but she refused. She and Rick had chosen Rambling Rose together, and despite being essentially alone in the small community, she never doubted that she belonged there.

Her girls were sixteen months old now, and life as a single mother hadn't exactly been a cakewalk. Rick's small life insurance policy had covered funeral expenses and allowed her to make her mortgage payments each month, but there hadn't been much left once she covered the essentials.

Not that she needed much for herself, but she wanted to give her daughters a good life. This job would go a long way toward her goal, but not if she messed it up by making a fool of herself before the center even opened.

Which was what she'd almost done with Callum Fortune. She hadn't been lying about missing breakfast, but her light-headedness had more to do with her reaction to the handsome stranger who'd come to her rescue.

Between work and caring for her girls, Becky hadn't even realized her heart could still flutter the way it did when Callum's dark gaze met hers. Butterflies had danced across her stomach and she'd had a difficult time pulling air into her lungs. Most women probably had the same inclination toward Callum. He would have been a standout in a big city like Dallas or Houston, but in the tiny town of Rambling Rose he was like a Greek god come to life.

Even now, her heart stuttered as she watched him smile at Ellie. Then his gaze tracked to hers, as if he could feel her eyes on him. His expression didn't change but there was something about the way he looked at her that made awareness prick along her skin. Dropping her gaze, she shoved a hand in the diaper bag that hung off the back of the stroller and pulled out a plastic container of dried cereal. The girls immediately perked up and she sprinkled a few oat bits into the stroller's tray before shoving a handful into her mouth. She really did need to remember breakfast.

Certainly an empty stomach was to blame for her dizziness, not the way Callum made her feel.

They cut the ribbon and the crowd, made up mostly of new employees of the center, cheered.

Luna clapped her hands at the noise while Sasha's chin trembled.

"It's okay, sweetie." Becky bent down and dropped a soothing kiss on her shy girl's cheek. "It's happy noise."

Sasha's big eyes widened farther as she looked around but after a moment she let out a sigh and settled back against the seat.

Meltdown averted. At least for now.

With twins, Becky rarely went for any long period without some sort of minor toddler crisis, but she wouldn't change a thing about either of her girls.

Callum and the rest of the pediatric center's VIPs had disappeared into the main lobby by the time Becky straightened.

"I hear they have cupcakes inside," a woman said as she passed Becky. "Your girls might like one."

"They're a little young for cupcakes," Becky answered with a laugh. "But I could use a treat."

"Those Fortune men are a treat for the eyes," the older woman said, giving Becky a quick wink. "If I were twenty years younger and not married…"

Becky was plenty young but also far too exhausted to consider dating. At least the fact that she could appreciate Callum's movie-star good looks proved motherhood hadn't destroyed her girlie parts completely.

As they approached the entrance, the woman asked, "You're the one who lost her husband a couple of years ago, right?"

She nodded, considering the joys and pitfalls of living in a small town.

"It's good you stayed in Rambling Rose. We take

care of our own. I'm Sarah. My husband, Grant, is the building manager for the pediatric center." The automatic doors whooshed open, and they walked into the lobby together. "Our kids are grown and moved away, so I've got more time on my hands than I can fill right now. If you ever need help—"

"Thank you," Becky said, forcing a smile. "I appreciate the offer, but I've got things under control."

Sarah gave her a funny look but nodded. "I understand. If you change your mind, Grant can get you my number."

Becky kept the smile fixed on her face until the woman walked away, then pressed two fingers to her forehead and drew in a steadying breath. She'd received at least a dozen similar offers since the twins' birth and had rejected every one. She hadn't really lied to Sarah. At this exact moment, she did have things under control. The girls were both sitting contentedly in the stroller watching the crowd.

Of course, things could go south at any moment. She'd handle that, too, on her own. She took the girls to a day care center when she worked, but otherwise didn't like to accept help. It had been her choice to stay in this town where she had no family. She didn't want people to think she was some kind of over-her-head charity case, even though most days she felt like she was treading water in the middle of the ocean.

But she didn't focus on that. She just kept her legs and arms moving so that she wouldn't go under. Her girls deserved the best she had to give, and she wouldn't settle for offering them anything less.

She was pushing the stroller toward the refreshment table when someone stepped in front of her path.

"Cupcake?" Callum Fortune asked.

Becky's mouth went suddenly dry, but she took the iced pastry from him. "Thanks," she whispered, then cleared her throat. "You did a great job with the building."

He shrugged but looked pleased by the compliment. "I love rehabbing old spaces, and this one is special."

"Ellie mentioned in her speech that the building used to house an orphanage." Becky took a small bite of cupcake and failed to smother a sigh of pleasure. It tasted so good.

Callum grinned. "Breakfast of champions," he told her with a wink. "And, yes. It was called Fortune's Foundling Hospital and dated back to the founding of Rambling Rose."

"Your family's ties to the town go back that far?"

"Apparently. I'll admit I'm still getting caught up on all the different branches of the Fortunes spread across Texas."

"You're royalty here," she told him, but he shook his head.

"Not me. I'm just a guy who loves construction."

"I think you're more than that." As soon as the words were out of her mouth, she regretted them. Somehow they sounded too familiar. People surrounded them, but for Becky the thread of connection pulsing between her and Callum gave the moment an air of intimacy that shocked and intrigued her.

His mouth quirked into a sexy half grin. "I appreciate—"

Suddenly, a woman burst into the lobby, clutching her very round belly. "Help me!" she cried. "I think I'm in labor."

"Get a gurney," Dr. Green shouted, elbowing his way through the crowd.

Becky took an instinctive step forward. Panic was clear on the woman's delicate features, and Becky understood that panic could accompany childbirth. But she couldn't leave her girls unattended.

Dr. Green straightened, his gaze searching the crowd until it alighted on her. "Becky, I need you," he called across the lobby.

She nodded and turned to Callum.

"I've got the girls," he told her without missing a beat. "Go."

She worked to calm her racing heart as adrenaline pumped through her. "Are you sure?"

She gave each of the girls a quick kiss and the assurance that Mommy would be back soon, then hurried toward the first patient in her new job.

"They're safe with me," he assured her, and although she'd just met Callum Fortune, she didn't doubt him for a moment.

Chapter Two

"Who knew Callum was such a spectacular nanny?" Steven asked an hour later, chuckling at his own joke.

Callum fought the urge to give his older stepbrother and business partner the one-fingered salute. Two adorable toddlers watched him from where they sat on a blanket he'd spread out in the pediatric center's lobby, so he wasn't about to model that kind of behavior.

The ribbon-cutting attendees had long since departed, the celebration cut short by the arrival of the pregnant stranger. Neither Parker Green nor the girls' mother had made an appearance again, and he wondered at the fate of the soon-to-be mom and her baby.

"We all know Callum is amazing with babies and children," Marci told Steven. "I'm not sure what I would have done without him when you all were little."

Steven was one of Marci's two sons from her first

marriage, but Callum's father had adopted both boys shortly after marrying his mother. The blended family had felt strange at first, but Stephanie's birth had solidified the bond they all shared. When Callum's construction business started to grow, Steven had joined him as a business partner, with Dillon coming on board soon after that. He'd changed the company name to more aptly describe their partnership, and Fortune Brothers Construction was still going strong.

"He'll be a great father one day," Callum's dad added with a knowing nod, prompting Steven and Callum to share an equally exasperated look. It was no secret their parents were intent on seeing both siblings happily married and starting families of their own.

Callum hadn't discussed future plans with his brother but got the impression Steven was as reluctant to settle down as Callum.

Stephanie walked through the doors that led to the center's small cafeteria. "I found plastic cups and spoons," she said. Callum had sent her in search of items to entertain the twins.

He took the makeshift toys and began stacking cups. The more confident of the girls, Luna, clapped her hands as if encouraging him to continue. He handed her a plastic spoon, which she waved in the air like a magic wand. One of the other nurses had told him the twins' names and that their mother was Becky Averill.

He'd asked about calling a husband and had been shocked to learn that Becky was a widow and single mom. It made him feel like even more of a heel for chastising her about breakfast. Becky was clearly an amazing woman, raising two children on her own while balancing a demanding career. No wonder she forgot to eat.

The shy twin, Sasha, scooted toward him. He held out a spoon to her, his chest tightening when her bottom lip trembled.

"Don't cry, darlin'," he told her softly and then scooped her into his arms. It had been an instinctual move. Callum had held plenty of babies when his sisters were younger. Sasha went rigid in his arms. Had he made a huge mistake? Then she relaxed against him with a quiet sigh, smelling like baby shampoo and oat cereal.

The front doors opened and two paramedics strode in. A moment later, Becky appeared from the medical clinic wing of the center. She and Dr. Green were wheeling out the pregnant stranger. The woman, a pretty brunette with big blue eyes, kept her worried gaze fixed on Becky, who appeared to be talking the patient through whatever was happening now.

There was no baby, and the woman seemed stable, so Callum could only assume things were good. Glancing over, Becky's expression softened as she caught sight of her twins. She said something to the pregnant patient, offered a quick hug and then walked toward Callum.

"How is she?" Stephanie asked immediately.

"We've given her something to slow her labor," Becky explained. "The baby's vitals are good, but Dr. Green thinks it will be better for her to give birth at a facility with a NICU. The paramedics are going to take her to San Antonio."

Callum's father nodded. "So she and the baby will be okay?"

"They should both come out of this healthy," Becky told them.

"Thank heavens," Marci added.

Callum stood, still holding Sasha in his arms. "It's a good thing you and Parker were here for the ribbon cutting."

"Dr. Green was essential," Becky clarified. "Anyone could have done what I did." She held out her hands, and Sasha reached for her, leaving Callum with an unfamiliar sense of emptiness.

"I doubt that's true," he answered. "You stepped in to help that woman without hesitation."

"I also foisted my kids off on you, and I appreciate you volunteering to watch them." She glanced down at Luna, who was still happily occupied with the spoon and cups, and then gave him a hesitant smile. "I'm Becky, by the way."

"One of the nurses told me," he said, that small smile doing funny things to his insides.

"You volunteered?" Marci stepped forward, patting Callum's shoulders. "I'm so proud."

"It wasn't a big deal," he mumbled.

"Your daughters are adorable," she said to Becky. "I'm Marci Fortune." She gestured to Callum's father and siblings. "My husband, David, and our daughter, Stephanie." Her smiled widened. "You know Callum, obviously. These are two of our other sons, Dillon and Steven."

Becky's caramel-colored eyes widened a fraction. "How many kids do you have?"

"Eight," Marci said proudly and without hesitation. Callum had always appreciated that his stepmother never differentiated between the children who were hers biologically and the two boys she'd taken on after marrying David.

"Wow," Becky murmured. "You must have been really busy."

"It's how we liked it," Marci assured her. She put a hand on Callum's arm. "Callum was such a help with his younger sisters. We also have triplets—Ashley, Megan and Nicole."

Dillon stepped forward. "Callum's nickname was Mary Poppins," he said in a not-so-quiet whisper.

Stephanie laughed while Becky tried to smother her smile.

"No one called me that," Callum told his brother with an eye roll. "Don't you all have somewhere to be?"

"You'd think with eight children," Marci said to Becky, ignoring Callum's question, "that we'd have a few grandchildren already."

"Gotta go," Dillon announced in response.

"Me, too," Steven added.

Stephanie grabbed her eldest brother's elbow. "I'll walk out with you."

Callum silently cursed his siblings as each of them gave Marci a peck on the cheek, told Becky it was nice to meet her and then quickly made their escape.

"You know how to clear a room, dear," David said, wrapping an arm around his wife's slim shoulders.

Marci only laughed. "I'd be an amazing grammy."

"Someday," her husband promised. "But we should go, too. We have a long drive to the airport."

Luna had lost interest in the makeshift toys and pulled herself up, then toddled over to Becky, who lifted her without missing a beat. "You aren't from Texas?" she asked Callum's parents.

David shook his head. "Fort Lauderdale, Florida. We flew in to see Callum's latest success. It's been quite an adjustment having four of our children move halfway across the country."

"The pediatric center is amazing," Becky said, glancing at Callum from beneath thick lashes. "It's lovely that you came all this way."

"Are you close to your parents?" Marci asked her.

Callum gave his father a look over the top of his stepmother's head. As much as he loved his big family, their friendly exuberance could be overwhelming. He didn't want to scare off Becky before he'd even had a chance for a proper conversation with her.

Before Becky could answer, David reiterated the need to get to the airport.

"I'll walk you out," Callum told them, then reached out and touched a hand to one of Luna's wispy curls. "Becky, I'll be right back."

She gave a quick nod, then seemed shocked when Marci leaned in and enveloped both her and the twins in a hug.

Marci turned to Callum at the entrance of the pediatric center. "She seems like a lovely girl," she said, her tone purposefully light.

"She's a single mother of twins," Callum felt obliged to point out. "And a widow."

"Tragic," Marci agreed as they walked into the cool January day. "I feel for those babies and for her. She deserves to find happiness again."

"It's not with me," Callum said. "I've committed to staying in Rambling Rose until the final project wraps up. Who knows what will happen beyond then?"

"I like this town more than I expected to," his father

interjected. "Of course, we'd love to see you back in Florida or somewhere closer, but if Texas makes you happy, that's most important."

"What about your mandate that we stay away from the Fortunes?"

David quirked a brow. "The only Fortunes in Rambling Rose are you and your siblings. I can live with that."

Callum walked them to the black sedan his father had rented. "Thank you both for coming to the opening." He hugged Marci first and then his father. "I'm proud of what we've accomplished here in such a short time."

"You should be," his father said.

"We're proud of you, as well," Marci added. "We always have been. But you work too much, Callum. Don't forget to take some time for yourself."

He didn't bother to argue. They wouldn't understand that his career fulfilled him in a way nothing else had. He knew people considered him a workaholic. Hell, that had been the main cause of his divorce. His ex-wife, Doralee, couldn't accept his hours or his dedication to the projects he managed.

But nothing made him happier than revitalizing older and historic commercial districts.

They said another round of goodbyes, and his parents climbed into their car and drove out of the parking lot.

As he walked back toward the entrance, Becky emerged, pushing the stroller.

"Thank you again," she said as he caught up to her. "I'd really like to repay you for your help today."

"No need." He held up his hands. "Thanks for stepping in with that woman. She seemed so terrified when she walked into the center."

A shadow seemed to darken Becky's delicate features. "She was scared and alone," she said, almost to herself. "And about to take on the greatest responsibility of her life."

"She didn't have a boyfriend or husband somewhere?" he couldn't help but ask. He fell in step next to Becky as she walked toward a nondescript minivan at the edge of the parking lot.

"Not that she'd tell us." She once again tucked her hair behind an ear and glanced over at him. "No family, either. I know how it feels to be alone, but there was something different about her. It was as if she was a speck of dandelion fluff floating in a breeze with no place to land." She let out a soft laugh. "I'm sure that sounds silly, but the woman—Laurel was her name— seemed like she really wanted to find a place to land."

"It sounds insightful," Callum murmured. In a single instant, his attraction to Becky Averill had gone from a physical spark to something more, something deeper.

"Sleep deprivation has robbed me of too many brain cells to be considered insightful." She pulled a key fob out of her bag and used it to open the minivan's side doors and cargo hold. "But I do feel for Laurel. I hope she and her baby flourish wherever she ends up."

Callum wanted to offer to do something to help with the twins and their stroller, but he felt like he needed to keep his distance. He'd been totally astounded by this woman today, but he had no place in her life and nothing to offer her. If his ex-wife had accused him of working too much, what would a single mother think of his crazy hours?

It didn't matter, he reminded himself as Becky turned to him with a tentative smile. "Are you sure there's no way I can thank you for today?" she asked. "I'm a pretty good cook and—"

"It's fine," he said, realizing how harsh he sounded only when her brows furrowed. "It was nice to meet you, Becky." He made his tone friendly but neutral. "You have cute kids." Without waiting for a response, he turned and walked away.

Becky finished with her final patient of the day, a three-year-old with double ear infections, and glanced at her watch as she walked toward the nursing station.

"Girl, you've been holding out on us." Sharla, one of the medical assistants in the primary care wing of the pediatric center, wagged a finger in Becky's direction. "We just heard Callum Fortune was your babysitter when that pregnant lady came in during the ribbon-cutting shindig."

Becky willed her face not to heat, but felt a blush rising to her cheeks anyway. This was her third shift at the center, and so far she'd loved every minute of it. Dr. Green, or Parker, as he insisted she call him when they weren't with patients, was an intelligent and caring physician. He had a rapport with both children and their parents, and Becky could see he took the utmost care with every patient.

Sharla and the other two nurses, Kristen and Samantha, were friendly and easy to talk to, and they all had good things to say about the doctors at the center. Becky had worked in enough different offices to appreciate the setup here.

"He offered to help," she said with what she hoped was a casual shrug. "It wasn't a big deal."

"Are you blind?" Kristen asked. "That man is ten kinds of a big deal."

"His brothers are just as hot," Samantha added.

"They aren't as handsome as Callum." Becky couldn't help the comment. Yes, the Fortune family had won the genetic lottery, but only Callum made her heart race. Every time she thought of the intensity of his dark gaze, her body seemed to heat from the inside out.

Sharla let out a peal of laughter. "I knew you had to notice."

"I'm a single mom," Becky muttered. "Not dead."

"So what are you going to do about it?" Kristen asked.

"There's nothing to be done." Becky placed the digital device she used for electronically entering patient data on the charging station. She wasn't going to admit to these three women that she'd offered to repay him for his kindness and he'd all but bolted from her.

Maybe it had been the minivan or her silly musings about the pregnant stranger or the reality of a woman with two toddlers in tow. Any one of those would have been a turnoff to a man. Add to that her reputation in town as the grieving widow and it was no wonder Callum had made a quick exit.

She'd obviously mistaken the intriguing thread of attraction between them or it had been all one-sided. No one would blame her for harboring a few harmless fantasies about a man like Callum, but that's all they were.

"My brother's insulation company is working on all of the Fortune Brothers Construction projects." Kristen tapped a finger to her chin, her green eyes sparkling. "I could get him to tell me when Callum is at one of the job sites and you could make an appearance there. He said all three Fortune brothers are really hands-on."

Sharla laughed again. "I'd like some Fortune hands on me."

Becky shook her head while the other two women joined in the joke. "I can't just show up at some construction site. What am I going to say? Remember me and will you hold one of my babies while I change the other one's dirty diaper?"

"Not the best pickup line I've heard," Samantha admitted.

Becky hadn't ever used a line on a man. Rick had been her first boyfriend. They'd met at freshmen orientation and dated through college, waiting to get married until after graduation because that's what her family wanted. He'd been an only child and not really close to his parents, who lived on the East Coast. Her mom and dad had expected her to hold off on marriage even longer, and their constant reminder that she and Rick had their whole lives to settle down had irritated Becky from the start. If she knew then what she did now, she would have married him right away so that they could have had more time together as a family.

No one could have predicted the car accident that had killed him, and Becky would always be grateful for the years he'd been a part of her life. But often she stayed busy, gave everything she had and more, because she was afraid if she ever stopped moving it might be too difficult to get up again.

"I'm not interested anyway," Becky lied. "I have too much going on to think about—"

"He's here," Sharla whispered.

All three of Becky's coworkers glanced at a place directly behind her, then quickly busied themselves.

As the fine hairs along the back of her neck stood on end, Becky turned around and came face-to-face with Callum Fortune.

"Hello," he said, running a hand through his thick mane of wavy dark hair. "I hope I'm not interrupting." He was dressed more casually today in a blue button-down shirt, dark jeans and cowboy boots. Callum looked perfect and she was painfully aware of her messy bun and the shapeless scrubs that were her work uniform. She glanced down to see some sort of crusty stain—probably baby spit-up—on her shoulder. Great. He looked like he owned the place, which he sort of did, and she was a scattered mess.

"Nope." Becky cleared her throat when the word came out a squeak. "I'm just finishing my shift and about to pick up the girls from day care."

She gave herself a mental head slap. Like he needed a reminder that she was a single mom with two young daughters.

"I'll walk with you," he offered.

"Oh." She stood there for a moment, trying to remember how to pull air in and out of her lungs.

"You remember where the day care's located, Becky?" Sharla asked from behind her. "Far end of the building and to the right."

She narrowed her eyes as she glanced at the other woman. "I remember. Thanks."

Callum offered a friendly smile as they started down the hall. "How's work going?"

"It's great," she said. "The facility is really great. The staff has been—"

"Great?" he asked with a wink.

"Sorry," she said automatically. "I'm always a little brain dead at the end of the day."

"Understandable. I can't imagine balancing everything you handle."

"It's not a big deal." She hated drawing attention to her situation. Becky found that the best way to stave off being overwhelmed was not to think about it. "I like to stay busy. What brings you to the center?"

She frowned as Callum seemed to stiffen next to her. Had she said the wrong thing again?

"Um... I needed to check on...some stuff."

"Sounds technical."

That drew a smile from him, and she felt inexorably proud that she'd amused him, even in a small way.

"I didn't mean to rush off the other day after the ribbon cutting," he told her as they approached the door that led to the child care center. "I think I interrupted a potential invitation for dinner, and I've been regretting it ever since."

Becky blinked. In truth, she would have never had the guts to invite Callum for dinner. She'd been planning to offer to cook or bake for him and drop it off to his office as a thank-you. The idea of having him to her small house did funny things to her insides.

"Oh," she said again.

"Maybe I misinterpreted," Callum said quickly, looking as flummoxed as she felt. "Or imagined the whole thing. You meant to thank me with a bottle of wine or some cookies or—"

"Dinner." She grinned at him. Somehow his discomposure gave her the confidence to say the word. He appeared so perfect and out of her league, but at the moment he simply seemed like a normal, nervous guy not sure what to say next.

She decided to make it easy for him. For both of them. "Would you come for dinner tomorrow night? The girls go to bed early so if you could be there around seven, we could have a more leisurely meal and a chance to talk."

His shoulders visibly relaxed. "I'd like that. Dinner with a friend. Can I bring anything?"

"Just yourself," she told him.

He pulled his cell phone from his pocket and handed it to her so she could enter her contact information. It took a few tries to get it right because her fingers trembled slightly.

He grinned at her as he took the phone again. "I'm looking forward to tomorrow, Becky."

"Me, too," she breathed, then gave a little wave as he said goodbye. She took a few steadying breaths before heading in to pick up the twins. *Don't turn it into something more than it is*, she cautioned herself.

It was a thank-you, not a date. Her babies would be asleep in the next room. Definitely not a date.

But her stammering heart didn't seem to get the message.

Chapter Three

Callum stood outside the soon-to-open veterinary clinic the following afternoon, frowning at the open back of the delivery truck.

"It's all pink," Stephanie reported.

"I see that," he answered, then turned to the driver. "We ordered modular cabinets in a pine finish."

"I just deliver what they give me," the man responded, scratching his belly. "Where do you want 'em?"

"Not here." Callum looked toward Steven, who was on his phone, pacing back and forth in front of the building's entrance.

His brother held up a finger and then returned to the phone call.

"This is a vet clinic." Stephanie gave a humorless laugh. "Not an ice cream parlor."

The cabinetry for the exam rooms and clinical areas had been ordered more than a month earlier. They needed it installed soon in order to keep the project on time and within budget. Callum and his brothers were sharing the responsibility of the vet clinic renovation, working with the staff of the local practice to design the space.

A moment later, Steven joined the group. "Take it back," he told the delivery driver before turning to Callum and Stephanie. "It was a clerical error. They typed in the wrong color code."

"Whatever you say, boss," the driver answered and pulled shut the overhead door of the delivery truck.

"It would have been my dream come true when I was eight," Stephanie said as the driver climbed into the vehicle and pulled away. "Working in a pink vet clinic."

"Where does that put us as far as the schedule?" Callum asked.

Steven's mouth tightened into a thin line. "I can get it done."

"I know that." Callum nodded, understanding that his older brother didn't appreciate being doubted. "I'm asking because if you need me to shift resources from other projects or change subcontractor timelines, we can make it work."

Steven's shoulders relaxed under his Western-style button-down shirt. "It's going to be tight. The supplier is putting a rush on the order so the cabinets should be here in two weeks. I can have the crew work on the flooring and finish the exterior. It's not ideal, but we'll make sure nothing falls behind."

"Let me know if we need to change our move-in date." Stephanie addressed them both. She not only worked at the current location of the vet center, but also acted as the liaison with the construction crew. "It's going to be all hands on deck at Paws and Claws to make it a smooth transition for our patients."

"Got it." Steven chuckled, then muttered, "Pink cabinets. We've had some strange setbacks, but that one might be the most colorful."

"If that's the worst unforeseen stumbling block in this whole process," Callum said, "I'll take it."

"The pediatric center opened without a hitch." Stephanie scrunched up her nose. "Other than a woman almost giving birth in the lobby."

Callum nodded. "I stopped by today, and the facility is already busy. Clearly there was a need for a children's health clinic in Rambling Rose."

"It feels like the town grows every day," Stephanie observed. "Have you noticed the new houses being built down the road from the ranch?"

Steven rubbed his thumb and fingers together. "Lots of money coming into the community. Hopefully that will mean plenty of business for each of our new ventures."

"Who needs a margarita?" Stephanie asked. "The pink cabinet fiasco made my head hurt, but it's nothing a salted rim along with a big plate of enchiladas won't cure."

"I'm in," Steven said.

Callum pulled out his phone and checked the time on the home screen. "I'll have to take a rain check. I have dinner plans tonight." He responded to a text from his foreman, then glanced up to find his brother and sister staring at him with equally curious expressions.

"Spill it," Stephanie said.

Callum feigned confusion. "What are you talking about?"

"He's evading answering." Steven elbowed their sister. "My money's on the cute nurse from the other day."

"He bombed out with her before he even got a chance," Stephanie said. "Tell me it's not that barista at the coffee shop in town who always flirts with you. She has crazy eyes."

"Enough with the inquisition." This was the issue with coming from such a close-knit family. Since they'd moved to Rambling Rose, he and his siblings had mostly hung out together. Sure, each of them had made a few casual friends. But they stuck together. The ranch they'd purchased just outside town had a sprawling main house as well as several guesthouses on the multiacre property.

He figured if his brothers and sister ever wanted more privacy in Rambling Rose, he'd buy out their portion of the ranch. But none of them seemed inclined to move out on their own anytime soon. It worked for Callum. He'd needed space after going to school at a local college in Florida. That was part of the reason he'd started looking for projects to take on in other areas of the Southeast. Coming from such a big family and growing up with so much responsibility for Stephanie and the triplets on his shoulders, he'd needed a break.

But after the wreck of his short marriage and subsequent divorce, life had become too quiet. Now he liked being close to his siblings. It had made the move to Texas not so daunting and gave him a sense of confidence, which was probably why he'd taken on a slate of so many ambitious projects.

"Then tell us," Stephanie prodded. "Don't think I

won't follow you. Remember when I was in eighth grade and crashed your date with Ava Martin after you snuck out to meet her?"

"How could I forget?" he replied, trying and failing to hide his smile. "I got grounded for a month."

"You were already grounded, which is why you got in even more trouble."

"No one is going to ground me now," he told her.

"Come on, Callum. Just spill it."

"I'm having dinner with Becky from the pediatric center."

"Called it." Steven did an enthusiastic fist pump. "You were so obvious the other day."

"I wasn't obvious," Callum said through clenched teeth. "I was helpful, and she's thanking me with dinner."

"How romantic," Stephanie said in a singsong voice.

"Her twins will be sleeping in their bedroom. It's hardly romantic."

"Mom and Dad had four boys under the age of five when they were first married," Steven reminded them. "They still managed to find some time for romance."

"This isn't anywhere near the same thing, and you both know it. You're just trying to get under my skin."

Stephanie wiggled her eyebrows. "It's working, too. I can tell." She leaned closer. "I can also tell you like her. You were pretty obvious at the ribbon cutting."

"Go back to Florida," he told her, deadpan.

"I'm like a rash," she countered. "You can't get rid of me."

Steven laughed. "You do realize you just compared yourself to a bad skin condition."

"Fitting," Callum said.

Stephanie only rolled her eyes at their gentle ribbing. "What are you bringing?"

Callum shrugged. "Nothing. She said she'd handle it all."

She groaned. "Don't be an idiot right out of the gate. What about flowers or wine or chocolate?"

"You sound like Marci," Callum told her. "Enough with the matchmaking."

"Li'l sis is right," Steven said. "Step up, Callum. Your pretty nurse has been through a lot. Even if it's just a thank-you, make her feel special."

"She's not 'my' anything," he protested, although his heart seemed to pinch at the thought of a woman like Becky belonging to him. He should listen to that subtle sharpening and not get any more involved with her when it could only end badly. "But she is special."

"Then show her," Steven urged, laughing when Stephanie gave him a playful slap. "Hey, what was that for? It's good advice."

"I'm just shocked it came from you."

"Remember, I'm the oldest." Steven pointed a finger at each of them. "That also means I'm the wisest."

"Hardly," Callum said on a half laugh, half cough. But his brother had a point. He didn't know much about Becky Averill, but it was obvious she worked hard, both at her job and taking care of her girls. She deserved to have someone treat her special. Despite knowing he could never be that man, he couldn't help wanting to ignore the truth—even for one night.

The doorbell rang at exactly seven o'clock that night.

Becky stifled a groan as she finished fastening the snaps on Luna's pajamas. "Of all the nights for things to go off the rails," she said to her girls as she lifted them into her arms and hurried toward the front of the small house.

She opened the door to Callum, who stood on the other side holding the most beautiful bouquet of colorful flowers she'd ever seen. "Am I early?" he asked, his dark gaze taking in the twins as well as Becky's bedraggled appearance.

"Bedtime is running late," she answered.

Luna babbled at him and swiped a chubby hand at the flowers while Sasha snuggled more deeply against Becky's shoulder.

"What can I do?"

Her heart did that melty thing she couldn't seem to stop around this man. "Give me five minutes," she told him as she backed into the house. "This night is to thank you for helping the first time, not to force you into another round of child care duties."

"I don't mind," he assured her, grinning at the girls.

"The flowers are beautiful," she said.

"They're for you." He looked down at the bouquet, then up at her again. "You probably guessed that."

Despite her nerves and the craziness of the evening, Becky grinned. "I have a bottle of wine on the counter. Would you open it while I put them down?"

"Sure."

It felt a bit strange to leave him alone in her house when he'd just arrived, but she didn't have a choice.

She began to sing softly to the girls as she made her way back to their bedroom. As if on cue, both Luna and Sasha yawned when Becky turned off the overhead light in the room, leaving the space bathed in only the soft glow from the butterfly night-light plugged in next to the rocking chair in the corner.

She placed them in their cribs, smiling as they babbled to each other in that secret language they seemed to share. She finished the song, gave each one a last kiss and said good-night. After checking the monitor that sat on the dresser, she quietly closed the door to their room.

Once in the hallway, she glanced down at herself and cringed. The twins were normally asleep by six thirty so Becky had thought she'd have a few minutes to freshen up before Callum arrived. She'd changed from her scrubs into a faded T-shirt and black leggings, both of which were wet thanks to the dual tantrums she'd dealt with during bath time.

Hurrying to her bedroom, she changed into a chunky sweater and dark jeans, cursing the fact that she hadn't been shopping for new clothes since before the girls were born. She hadn't done anything for herself in far too long, which was why this night felt so special.

She dabbed a bit of gloss on her lips, fluffed her hair and headed for the kitchen and Callum. Her heartbeat fluttered in her chest once again.

Her reaction to his presence felt silly. He'd helped with her daughters and agreed to come for dinner. Nothing more. He probably regretted it already and was counting the minutes until he could make his escape.

But the warmth in his gaze when he looked up from his phone as she walked into the kitchen told a different story. One that made sparks tingle along her spine.

"You arranged the flowers," she murmured, taking in the bouquet that had been placed in a vase on the table.

"I found a vase in the cabinet." He offered a sheepish smile. "I hope you don't mind. It was one less thing you'd have to deal with tonight."

"They're perfect," she told him, then breathed out a soft laugh. "You can manage multiple construction projects and excel at the art of floral arranging. Quite the Renaissance man, Callum."

Her silly comment seemed to relax them both. She could hardly believe he had nerves in the same way she did, but the thought made her feel more confident.

"Something smells really great," he told her.

"I almost forgot about dinner," she admitted, pulling a face. "It's not fancy, but I hope you like chicken potpie."

"I like everything."

And didn't those words just whisper across her skin like a promise? Becky gave herself a little head shake. He was talking about food and she stood there staring at him like he was the main course.

"My grandma used to make it when we went to her house for Sunday dinner. I make some modifications so the recipe doesn't take so long, but the crust is homemade."

"I'm impressed." He handed her a glass of wine. "To new friends and new beginnings."

She clinked her glass against his and took a drink of the bright pinot grigio. It was only a sip but she would have sworn the tangy liquid went right to her veins, making her feel almost drunk with pleasure.

More likely the man standing in her kitchen caused that. The first man who'd been there with her since her husband's death.

"New beginnings," she repeated softly, then busied herself with dinner preparations.

She'd done most of the work when she got home earlier. The pie was warm in the oven, and the scent of chicken and savory dough filled the air when she took it out and set it on the trivet she'd placed on the kitchen table.

She took a salad from the refrigerator, then frowned at the simple supper. Surely a man like Callum was used to fancier fare.

"I haven't cooked for ages," she admitted as she joined him at the table. "I'm out of practice at entertaining."

As if understanding there was an apology implicit in her words, Callum shook his head. "This looks amazing, and I appreciate you going to the trouble for me."

"It was no trouble." She dished out a huge helping of the classic comfort food onto his plate. "I hope you're hungry."

As he took a first bite, he closed his eyes and groaned in pleasure. "I could eat this every night."

"I used to make things that were more gourmet, but with the girls' bedtime routine I figured I'd have better luck with a recipe I know by heart."

"I'm not much for gourmet."

"That surprises me." She forked up a small piece of crust, pleased that it tasted as good as she remembered. "I figured anyone with the last name of Fortune would be accustomed to the finer things in life."

"Nothing finer than a home-cooked meal," he said, helping himself to another portion.

She chuckled. "Do you always eat so fast?"

"Only when it's this good." He shrugged. "My branch of the family is relatively new to the notoriety of the Texas Fortunes."

"Really? Is that why you moved here? To get your moment in the spotlight?" She mentally kicked herself when he grimaced. He'd helped her and now her nerves had her babbling so much she was going to offend him. "I'm sorry. That came out sounding rude."

"Rambling Rose appealed to me because I'm here in Texas, which gives me a sense of connection with the Fortune legacy, but it also feels like I'm blazing my own path."

"That's important to you?" She stabbed a few pieces of lettuce with her fork.

"Very important. You met my dad and stepmom and three of my siblings. Imagine four more added to the mix. There wasn't much time for individuality growing up. I could hardly do my own thing when I constantly had a brother or younger sister trailing me."

"Are you the oldest?"

He studied his plate for a long second, as if unsure how to answer. "No. Dillon, who was at the ribbon cutting ceremony, is a year younger than me. Our parents divorced when I was a toddler, and Dad met Marci shortly after. They married almost immediately. She also had two boys from her first marriage. Steven is two years older and Wiley is my age, although he has a couple of months on me. It felt like I went from being the oldest to the little brother overnight."

"That's a lot of blending," Becky murmured, not quite able to imagine how that would have felt for a young boy.

He nodded. "We were a handful, especially at the beginning. I think each of us had something to prove. Unfortunately that meant we pushed every one of Marci's buttons any chance we got."

"How did she handle it?"

"Like a champ," Callum confirmed. "I didn't see my real mom much after the divorce, but Marci always made Dillon and me feel like we were her sons as much as Steven and Wiley. If we were testing her, she passed with flying colors."

"And things got easier?"

"Stephanie was a turning point for the family. She was the most precious thing I'd ever seen. Suddenly, these four rowdy boys had something in common—our sister. She brought us together."

"It's obvious you're close with her."

"Yeah." The softening of his features gave her that fizzy feeling again. "Mom…" He cleared his throat. "Marci became mom to me pretty quickly. She loved having a big family, but had a couple of pregnancies that ended in miscarriage after that. It took a toll on her."

"I can imagine."

Fine lines bracketed his mouth, as if the thought of the woman who'd become a mother to him hurting caused him physical pain, as well.

"Then the triplets were born. They were miracle babies, really."

"Multiples are special," Becky couldn't help but add, thinking of her sweet girls.

"It took Marci some time to recover. There were complications and she wasn't herself for a while after."

"From how she made it sound, you were a huge help."

His big shoulders shifted and an adorable flush of color stained his cheeks. "I kind of had a way with the ladies, even back then."

Laughter burst from Becky's mouth, and the excitement bubbling up in her felt like she'd gulped down a flute of champagne. Was there anything more attractive to a mother than a man who was good with children?

"You certainly worked your charms on Luna and Sasha," she told him. "They aren't accustomed to having men in their lives."

"Someone told me your husband died while you were pregnant," Callum said quietly. "I'm sorry."

The pleasure rippling through her popped in an instant. Grief had been a sort of companion to her after Rick's death, and she knew the facets of it like the back of her hand.

"It was a car accident," she said. "I'd just taken a home pregnancy test but we didn't know I was carrying twins." She bit down on the inside of her cheek. "I wish I could have shared that with him. I wish I could have shared a lot of things."

She held up a hand when he would have said more because she knew another apology was coming. Not that he had any responsibility, obviously, but people didn't know how to talk to her about the loss she'd suffered. Some things were too unfathomable for words.

"We're okay," she said, which was her pat line even when it wasn't true. Sometimes she struggled, but she was dealing with it and making the best of things for her daughters. She blinked away the tears that stung the backs of her eyes.

"In some ways Rick is still with us," she told Callum. "There's a park outside of town where he and I used to go on walks after work. Now I take Luna and Sasha there when I want to feel close to him. I sit on the bench near the pond and talk to him, and I feel him with us. I know how much he would have loved his girls and he's their guardian angel. Some people don't get that or they think I'm just trying to see the silver lining in a tragedy that has none. But it's what I know."

His cleared his throat as if unsure how to respond. Becky mentally kicked herself. No guy wanted to spend an evening talking about a woman's dead husband, even for a homecooked meal. This was the reason she could never hope to date, especially not someone like Callum Fortune. She had enough emotional baggage to fill a freight train.

"Can I ask why you stayed in Rambling Rose?" Callum asked after several awkward moments.

She opened her mouth to give him a pat answer, but was somehow unable to tell this man anything but the complete truth. "This was the home Rick and I chose together." She glanced around the small kitchen. "And we picked this town because we wanted to be a part of a close-knit community. Neither of us was tight with our families growing up."

"Do you have brothers and sisters?"

She shook her head. "Only child. Rick was, too." She lifted the wineglass to her lips, watching Callum from beneath her lashes. Maybe it was inappropriate to talk about her late husband with a man she felt attracted to, but Callum's steady presence made her feel like she could share anything with him.

She appreciated that more than she could say. Yes, she'd loved her husband deeply and would give anything to change the tragedy that had stolen their future.

That loss was woven into the fiber of her being. It had formed her into the woman she was today, resilient and fiercely protective of her daughters. She understood the only way to celebrate Rick's life was by honoring what had brought her to this point.

Callum helped her clean up the dishes after they finished dinner, another point in his favor. They said goodbye, and Becky watched him drive away as she tried to tamp down the disappointment at the night ending so soon. Seriously, she needed to get out more. One simple thank-you dinner and she felt like a silly girl with a crush on the most popular boy at school.

Callum had called her a friend and that was how she should think of him, as well. Too bad her body wouldn't cooperate.

Chapter Four

"What's your next move?" Stephanie asked as she joined Callum in the main house's expansive kitchen later that week.

The morning had just begun to dawn, with the sky outside the window turning the Fame and Fortune Ranch a dozen shades of pink and orange.

"I don't have one," he said, keeping his gaze trained on his laptop. He took another drink of coffee as he perused the article on trends in the food and hospitality industry. "What would you think about an upscale restaurant in Rambling Rose?"

"I think it won't compete with the local Mexican food," she said, dropping into a chair across from him at the table.

"The idea isn't to compete," he explained. "I want to expand the options for folks around here. What if you wanted to go on a special date?"

"At this point," Stephanie said with a slightly sad smile that tugged at his heart, "my favorite men have four legs and fur."

Callum hated that his sister seemed to have given up on her chance at love. Unlike him, Stephanie had so much to give. "Hypothetically," he clarified.

"Are *you* looking for a setting for a special date?" Stephanie kicked his shin under the table. "You still haven't said anything about your dinner with Becky the other night. I'm tired of waiting for details."

"She's a great cook," he said.

"I don't care what you ate." Stephanie pushed his laptop closed. "You like her, right?"

"She's nice." Callum reached for his coffee, ignoring his sister's raised brow. Of course, *nice* was a wholly inadequate way to describe Becky. He'd never met anyone like her. She'd suffered a devastating tragedy yet still seemed to be filled with a bright light that wouldn't be dimmed.

He didn't understand the connection he felt with her and knew it could go nowhere even if he wanted it to. Which he didn't because he'd learned his lesson about commitment and getting hurt the hard way. Things were better all around when Callum focused on the parts of his life he could control. Matters of the heart definitely didn't fall into that category.

"What did you talk about?"

"Stuff."

"You know how persistent I can be," she said. "I'll follow you around all day until you spill it." Stephanie grinned when he narrowed his eyes. "Might as well just tell me now."

"We talked about a lot of things." He shrugged. "My family, her family. Her late husband."

She made a soft sound of distress. "Was that awkward?"

"No," he answered simply. Maybe it should have been. Although the way she'd described Rick made the man sound just about perfect. Callum knew he was bound to pale in comparison. There was no use pretending that he'd gone to dinner at Becky's just to be kind. He couldn't stop thinking about her.

He wasn't just attracted to her physically. He wanted to know as much as he could about her, which included her past. Losing a husband so young had obviously played a large part in shaping the person she was today.

"I haven't seen you like this since Doralee." Stephanie tapped a finger on the tabletop, and Callum focused his attention on that instead of meeting her insightful gaze.

"It isn't the same," he muttered.

"I can tell." She leaned forward until he lifted his gaze to hers. "Your divorce doesn't define you, Callum. At least it shouldn't."

"I know," he agreed, although the wreck of his marriage had changed him. All the things he'd thought he wanted from life shifted in the wake of his pain and the blame his ex-wife placed squarely on his shoulders.

He deserved every bit of it. Growing up in a large family had led him to assume the path of marriage and kids was the one that made the most sense for him. But he'd been dedicated to his business and not able to give Doralee the attention she'd wanted. They'd had a whirlwind courtship of only six weeks before getting married, both of them enamored by the heady feeling of new love.

Once the novelty wore off, it had become clear they weren't compatible in most of the ways that counted. She had unrealistic expectations and he seemed doomed to fail at meeting them. It was a blessing for both of them that she'd had the guts to end things. He hadn't wanted to hurt her but couldn't seem to do anything right. He'd believed he was building a future for the two of them, laying the groundwork for their life together. Turned out to be a foundation built on sand, shifting and crumbling under the pressures of life.

Of course his failings had shaped him, but in a different way from how Becky's had her. She'd had tragedy befall her and risen above it, while he'd been the cause of his own pain. He might be infatuated with her, but he wasn't about to open himself up to that kind of hurt again. Becky's life was complicated and he remained determined to keep his as simple as he could manage.

"You can find love again," Stephanie continued.

"I'm not looking for love." He pushed back from the table and walked toward the counter to refill his coffee. "It was one dinner. You're making too much of it."

"I know you, Callum. All I'm saying is don't shut the door on a possibility before you've given it a chance."

He paused with his hand on the coffeepot's handle. His sister was right, of course. He'd decided after his divorce that he valued his independence too much to make a committed relationship work. The decision hadn't been a problem because no one he'd met had made him question it.

Until Becky.

"When did you get too smart for your own good?" he asked.

Stephanie grinned. "I've always been brilliant. You're just realizing it."

"I'll keep that in mind," he said with a laugh. They talked some more about possibilities for an upscale restaurant in Rambling Rose, and then Callum headed out to start his morning.

He appreciated the pace of life in Texas. He could move quickly, but things also seemed to adjust to fit the wide-open spaces and the sense of community pride that felt uniquely Texan. This was a setting that made a man earn his place. The residents of Rambling Rose might be curious about his ties to the famous Fortune family, but people seemed more concerned with his dedication to the town.

Callum felt at home here in a way he hadn't during any of the other projects he'd taken on over the years. It made his desire to succeed burn even brighter and caused the future to beckon in ways he hadn't anticipated.

Later that week, Becky looked up from the lunch she'd packed to see Callum walking toward her across the pediatric center's sunny courtyard. A slow smile spread across her lips as awareness tingled along her spine. This was the third day Callum had appeared during her lunch break.

Maybe she shouldn't read too much into it. He'd explained he had business at the pediatric center. She had no reason not to believe him.

"What's on the menu today?" he asked as he slid into the seat across from her. Becky always took her lunch early since most mornings she didn't have time for breakfast.

"Turkey and cheese," she said, then pulled out the extra sandwich she'd made. "I have one for you if you're hungry."

He stared at the plastic baggie for so long she wasn't sure if he was going to take it or get up from the table and run the other direction. When he finally reached for the sandwich, it embarrassed her that she'd even made the effort to bring something extra for him. "Thank you," he said. "That's thoughtful."

Electricity zipped along her skin as his fingers brushed hers. Her reaction to Callum continued to surprise her. She couldn't remember a time when anticipation had played such a huge part in her life. Despite her busy work schedule and how much effort she put into mothering her girls, Becky felt like she had energy for days. Just the idea of seeing Callum at some point during the day had excitement zinging through her veins like a jolt of caffeine.

"Are you here checking on the mechanical systems again?" she asked.

"Um...yes."

"Will they have it fixed soon?" She pulled a container of apple slices from her lunch sack.

"Probably." He took a bite of sandwich. "Although I may need to stop by for a while longer to make sure it's all going well."

"That has to be frustrating. I'm sure you're ready to move on to your other projects."

"I like seeing how well things are going here," he told her, then leaned in close. "Talking with you is an added bonus."

"Oh." Heat bloomed in her cheeks. "That's nice."

She gave herself a mental head slap. A man said something sweet and her reply was completely boring. She imagined men like Callum came out of the womb knowing how to flirt, and Becky reminded herself that it didn't mean anything. That she didn't *want* it to mean anything.

"How are the girls?" he asked, grinning at her like she wasn't making an absolute hash of flirting with him.

"They're enjoying the new day care." She tugged her lower lip between her teeth. "I'd like to visit them during the day but the director told me it's too disruptive for their schedule."

"You're a dedicated mom," he murmured.

"Sasha and Luna are my whole world," she told him. That was probably the wrong thing to say, as well. What single man wanted to hear a woman gush over her children? But she couldn't deny it.

"Maybe I could take the three of you to dinner?" His smile turned almost bashful. "If you have a free night sometime?"

She clasped a hand over her mouth when a hysterical laugh bubbled up in her throat.

"What's so funny?"

"All of my nights with the girls are free. Unless you include dinner, bath time and reading board books as a busy schedule."

"So dinner would work?"

"Sure." She felt a frown crease her forehead. "Why would you want to subject yourself to a meal with two toddlers?"

He inclined his head as if pondering a response. "Um…we all need to eat and as great as my brothers and sister are, I sometimes need a little break from the family togetherness."

"I'm not sure dinner with the twins constitutes a break, but I won't say no to an evening out."

"How about tomorrow night?"

"Yes," she breathed, then cleared her throat. "Tomorrow would be great. I get off work at five, which I understand is early for dinner. But with the girls' bedtime…"

"Do you like the Mexican restaurant in town?"

"I haven't been there in ages," she told him with a smile, then gave a nervous laugh. "Not because I don't like it. I do. It's great. I haven't been anywhere, really." She covered her face with her hands, then spread her fingers to look at him. "I'm babbling."

"It's cute," he said, his tone soft like velvet. "You're cute, Becky."

"You're cute, too."

He chuckled. "No one has ever called me that."

She lowered her hands and arched a brow. "I bet you were an adorable baby. A handful, but adorable."

"Definitely a little terror," he agreed.

She sighed. "You have a way of making me jittery, then calming my nerves in the next instant."

"I'm glad."

"I'm glad you asked me to dinner," she said honestly.

"Me, too."

They sat in a charged silence for a long moment. His full lips quirked into a smile, and she wondered what it would be like to feel that mouth against hers. The desire zipping through her was a thrill. She longed to see where it might take her.

Nowhere fast, a voice inside her head warned. Not

with this man. She hushed that voice and offered Callum a wide smile. "I need to get back to work. I'll see you at the restaurant tomorrow?"

He stood as she did, leaning close to whisper in her ear. "I can't wait."

Her nerve endings buzzed with the pleasure of his breath tickling the fine hairs along her neck.

Not trusting herself to speak, she simply nodded, then grabbed her lunch sack and hurried toward the primary care wing.

She had a date with Callum Fortune.

Tomorrow couldn't come soon enough.

Later that evening, Callum stared at the familiar name on his cell phone's screen for a few seconds before accepting the call.

"Hey, Doralee," he said as he put the phone to his ear. "This is a surprise."

"Hello, Callum," his ex-wife said, her voice the same rasp he remembered. It seemed like a lifetime ago that they'd flown to Vegas and gotten married on a whim. He'd been young and in love, not exactly sure he was doing the right thing but willing to take a chance because he knew it would make her happy.

In the end, their rash decision had achieved the opposite effect. He'd always regret hurting her, even though it had never been his intention.

"It's good to hear from you," he lied, not sure how this conversation was supposed to go.

She laughed. "I don't believe you for a minute, but I still appreciate hearing it. How's Texas?"

"Big."

"Are the projects going well?"

"So far they are. There have been a few hiccups, but we're on schedule."

"No doubt thanks to your time and dedication."

He gripped the phone more tightly. "I can't tell if that's a compliment or a veiled criticism."

"You're the best at what you do," she answered without hesitation. "The rest of your life might take a hit because of it, but I'm sure you'll have as much success in that tiny town as you did back here."

"Thanks," he murmured. He didn't exactly appreciate her willingness to point out what he'd sacrificed for the sake of his career but he also couldn't deny it. "How are things?"

"Great." He heard her blow out a slow breath. "That's actually why I'm calling, Callum. I have some news that I wanted you to hear from me first."

His stomach pitched like he'd just raced down the first big drop on a roller coaster. "What news?" he asked, although he had a feeling he knew what she was going to say.

"I'm engaged."

"Congratulations," he said, forcing his tone to stay neutral. "I'm happy for you." That part wasn't a lie. He wanted the best for his ex-wife. Just because things hadn't worked out for the two of them didn't mean he'd stopped caring about her.

"I appreciate that," she said. "John is a great guy. He wants to start a family right away, and you know I wanted children."

"Yes," he managed before his throat constricted. Her desire to have children and his unwillingness to start a family had been one of their biggest ongoing arguments during their short marriage.

"It seems like we're both getting the lives we wanted," she continued. "You have a thriving business and I'm going to have a family."

When he didn't respond right away, she continued, "We're planning a spring wedding. Not that you care but like I said, I just wanted you to know."

He swallowed and tried to keep his regret over the past in check. "Please tell your fiancé I said congratulations."

"I will. Are you dating anyone?" she asked, but continued before he could answer. "Never mind. I already know the answer. Even if you're dating it isn't serious. The business is your first love and no one can compete with that."

He mumbled something about wishing her luck, and they ended the call. A thin sheen of sweat covered Callum's forehead.

Up until the moment of hearing Doralee's news, he would have also claimed his life was happy. But her comments about his devotion to his career, whether well-meaning observations or insidious slights, made his gut twist.

He didn't disagree with her assessment of his dedication to the company, but suddenly that seemed like a paltry excuse for the choices he'd made to avoid serious relationships since the divorce.

His ex-wife had moved on with someone who would probably make her far happier than Callum ever had. It was an unwanted but necessary reminder of what he was unwilling to give in a relationship, in large part due to the responsibilities he'd taken on as a child. He couldn't make that kind of commitment and the thought that he might be giving Becky the wrong signals made him doubt everything.

Should he cancel the date with Becky?

He couldn't play around with the emotions of a single mother, especially one who had survived the tragedy of losing her husband. In truth, it didn't feel like he was toying with her. Becky was like a Fourth of July sparkler come to life. Through everything she'd endured in life and how hard she worked to support her daughters, she practically sparkled with energy. She made him feel alive in a way that even his work hadn't for a long time.

Doralee had reminded him of how little he had to give, but thoughts of Becky inspired him to be more. To give more. To want more. If only he could be that man.

Chapter Five

Becky parked the minivan around the corner from Las Delicias, the Mexican restaurant situated on Rambling Rose's quaint main street. She remembered the first time she and Rick had made the trip to visit the town. She'd been charmed by the rustic beauty of the town, a little worn down and in need of some love but with so much potential and the feeling of home.

Now the man she'd agreed to meet for dinner was the one breathing new life into the community. It wasn't just the pediatric center. She knew Callum was working on a new vet clinic, an upscale shopping mall, a spa and even had plans for a boutique hotel. Up until his investment in the town, most of the money had been limited to the outskirts of the community. He lived in a wealthy enclave, but many of those residents kept to themselves, as if they didn't want to tarnish their fancy image by rubbing shoulders with the true locals.

Becky wasn't exactly a local, but she was raising two daughters who'd been born in the town. She appreciated that Callum didn't seem to care about the differences between them and that he wasn't intimidated by her situation.

Part of why she hadn't thought about dating in the past two years was her fear that a man would assume her twins were simply complications. Becky wasn't sure her heart could stand that.

She quickly checked her makeup in the visor's small mirror. Normally she didn't bother, but tonight she'd actually put some effort into her appearance. It had felt good, like she was some kind of single mom butterfly emerging from her chrysalis. With the help of a dab of concealer and a few subtle swipes of shadow, she looked more like the Becky she remembered and less like an exhausted, overworked mom.

The change made her smile.

"Mama," Luna shouted from the back seat. "Go."

"Go," Sasha repeated softly.

Her girls were learning new words every day, and Becky loved this time in their development. They were little sponges, soaking up everything and making even the most mundane parts of life an adventure.

But she couldn't deny that kids complicated dating, especially two squirming toddlers. Becky unstrapped the girls from their car seats, scooped them up and then slung the diaper bag over her shoulder. She hit the fob to close and lock the car just as Luna dived for her ring of keys. They fell from Becky's grasp and landed on the pavement, skittering underneath the vehicle.

"Uh-oh," Sasha said, her voice grave.

"Mommy will get them," Becky promised, cursing the pale yellow jeans she'd chosen for the evening. They'd seemed so fresh at her house, but this latest small catastrophe was the exact reason she normally didn't wear anything but jeans, scrubs or sweatpants.

"I've got it," Callum said, appearing at her side like some kind of superhero. He deftly crouched down to retrieve the keys, the fabric of his striped shirt stretching across the lean muscles of his back.

"Thanks," Becky said when he straightened again, wishing she could control the blush that seemed to appear every time he looked at her.

"My pleasure," he answered. "You ladies look lovely this evening." He held out his hands, and to Becky's surprise, Sasha reached for him.

"She usually doesn't let other people hold her." Becky's mouth went slack as Callum grinned at her shy daughter, then tucked an arm around her like it was the most natural thing in the world.

"Sasha and I have an understanding." He winked at Becky. "She's helping me win points with her mom."

"Very true." Becky returned his smile. "You have a way with babies." They started toward the restaurant. The evening was particularly mild for this time of year, and the fresh air helped to cool her heated cheeks.

"I had way too much experience in my own family."

The words were spoken lightly, but somehow she could sense that they meant more to him than he was letting on. If that was how he felt about children, what was he doing there with her and the twins?

"There were four brothers all around the same age, right?"

Callum nodded.

"I'm wondering why you were designated your step-mother's helper."

"It started with Stephanie," he said. "I had a connection with her from the start. I didn't even realize what I was taking on until it happened. There were things that Marci needed done with the baby, so I did them. Even if Stephanie was crying like crazy, she'd settle down once I played with her."

"I bet your parents appreciated that." Becky knew she would love that kind of baby whisperer.

"Yeah," he agreed. "They also came to rely on it in a way that none of us realized was too much for a kid my age to handle. The same thing happened when the triplets were born."

They'd reached the restaurant and he held open the door for her. The interior was a homey homage to south-of-the-border decor. Strands of lights hung against warm yellow walls, with colorful flags and sombreros rounding out the decorations. The place was more than half-full, which Becky thought was good for so early on a weeknight.

A stocky man with a pencil-thin mustache strode forward to greet them. "Mr. Fortune," he said, pumping Callum's free hand. "We have your table ready. What a beautiful group of women you have with you tonight."

"I'm a lucky man," Callum answered easily.

Becky felt the eyes of a pretty hostess behind the podium assessing her. Like Becky, the young woman probably wondered what Callum was doing out with a mom and two toddlers. Rambling Rose was a quiet town, but there were enough available women that he could have enjoyed an evening without a baby's sticky hands patting his cheeks, the way Sasha did to him now.

The man, who introduced himself as the restaurant's owner, led them to a table in a quiet corner, already set up with two high chairs. The girls, unaccustomed to dining out, looked around at their new surroundings with wide-eyed curiosity. She and Callum strapped each of them into a high chair, and she took out the travel toys she'd brought to entertain them. A waitress quickly brought water and took their drink orders before hurrying off again.

Becky smothered a giggle as she took a seat next to Luna. "I've never been treated like this at a restaurant," she admitted, glancing around to make sure no one could hear. "Even before I had the twins. Now on the few occasions I've tried to go out to eat with them it feels like the waitstaff resents every moment I'm taking up space. Must be nice to be a true VIP."

Callum blinked as if he'd never considered his elevated status or the perks that came with it. "Why would anyone mind if you had the girls with you?"

As if on cue, Luna chucked a wooden block across the table. Callum reached up and caught it without missing a beat.

"You just intercepted the first reason," Becky told him with another laugh. "There's also the distinct possibility of a meltdown by one or both of them. Not to mention more food falls on the ground than makes it into their mouths."

"People go out to eat with kids all the time," he countered. "It's no big deal."

She shrugged and glanced down at the menu. "Maybe I feel it more because I'm on my own. I don't get to tag out or divide the responsibility. I wouldn't change having twins, but it can be a lot. I'm sure that's why your stepmom ended up depending on you so much with the triplets."

The waitress returned to the table with a beer for Callum and a margarita for Becky. They ordered, and then Callum lifted his glass in a toast when they were on their own again.

"Tonight's toast is to you being the VIP for the night," he told her, the warmth in his gaze setting off an answering heat low in her belly. Luna lifted her sippy cup, and Callum gamely clinked his beer against her plastic cup and then Sasha's. "And a toast to me being with three very important ladies tonight," he said, making funny faces that had the girls squealing in delight.

Becky tried to shush them, but he seemed to enjoy the noise. She couldn't figure out Callum's contradictions. Although he clearly loved his family, it was just as obvious that he still harbored some resentment over the position he'd been put in as caregiver to his younger sisters. Why would he willingly get involved with her when he knew her situation?

She took a breath and put those thoughts aside.

It didn't matter why. She needed to just enjoy the evening.

They talked and laughed, and Callum continued to entertain her girls. When Sasha began to fuss, Becky pulled out a binky and the girl popped it in her mouth and sucked contentedly. Luna wasn't so easy to pacify, so Becky was grateful that the toddler appeared completely enamored of Callum.

Like mother like daughter.

Just as their food arrived, Luna decided she'd had enough of the high chair. Becky lifted the girl into her arms, a pro at eating one-handed.

"I forgot how good food tastes when you don't have to cook," she told Callum around a bite of chicken enchilada. "It's the closest I've had to gourmet in ages."

"What would you think of going out sometime, just the two of us?" he asked as he deftly caught the pacifier Sasha tossed at him. The girl offered a wide grin and put it back in her mouth when he returned it to her.

Becky tried not to react, but the words turned the yummy food she'd eaten into a lead balloon in her stomach.

"I'm sorry," she said automatically, still bouncing Luna on her knee. "This was a terrible idea." She pushed away her half-eaten plate of food and began gathering the girls' things into the diaper bag. "If you see the waitress, I'll take care of the check… It's the least I can do."

Callum covered her hand with his. "What's wrong? Did I say something?"

She shook her head as she stared at the back of his tanned hand and the smattering of fine hair covering it. His body was so different from hers, and just the thought of it made her heart swoop and dance.

But it didn't matter if he couldn't accept the reality of her life. "It's not you. It's me." She made a face. "That sounds like a line, but I mean it. This is why I haven't dated. The girls and I are a package deal. I get we're a lot, and I don't expect you to be okay with it. I just thought—"

"I know how dedicated you are to your daughters," he told her, squeezing her fingers gently. "Your unconditional love for them is one of the things I admire about you. I've never felt that way about anything or anyone. I'm not sure I have it in me."

"Then why are you suggesting I leave them behind?" She hated the catch in her voice and the tears that pricked the back of her eyes. The problem with loving her girls so darn much was that everything about them made her emotional. Or perhaps that was due to exhaustion or loneliness or the silly hope she'd allowed herself to have that Callum might not care about the tragedy that defined her life and her responsibilities as a mom.

"I'm not. I promise." He laced their fingers together, and the heat of his hand spread into all the cold, lonely places deep within her. "Of course I want to spend time with them. I just thought a night off would be good for you. Give you a little break."

"I don't need a break."

He traced tiny circles on the inside of her palm with his thumb. "Every mother I've ever known needs a break at some point. I'm not saying that because of how much I helped Marci growing up. You work full-time and dedicate every other waking minute to your daughters."

"They're my life."

He stared at her, and she found herself fidgeting under his perceptive gaze. "After Rick died," she said softly, "my parents pressured me to move back to Houston. When I refused, my mom told me I'd regret staying here on my own. She said if I didn't return home they wouldn't help me. I'd have to do everything on my own."

"I'm sure she was just angry and worried," he said.

"They haven't seen the twins since they were six months old."

"What about their first birthday?"

"I took them to the park on my own."

His thumb stopped moving.

"I don't understand," he told her. "These are their granddaughters."

Becky shrugged. "Maybe they'll come around eventually. It's not a big deal. The girls are too young to realize anything." She tugged her hand away from his when the waitress came to clear the plates. Luna's head drooped against her chest. "But I guess it's left me with something to prove. If I admit that I need time off from being a mom…" Her breath hitched, and she swallowed back the emotion that formed a ball in her throat. "That feels like failure."

Sasha gave a tiny cry, and Callum reached for her without hesitation. Becky tried and failed to stay unaffected by his easy way with the girls.

"You must know you're an amazing mother. Your girls are clearly happy and thriving."

She sniffed and busied herself loading the diaper bag while he managed to take out his wallet and then his credit card with one hand.

"I can take her," she offered, shifting Luna in her lap.

"All good." Callum waited until the waitress had taken his credit card to continue. "Tell me you know I wasn't trying to avoid being with Luna and Sasha."

"I know," she said with a nod. "I'm sensitive about them. About my status as a single mom."

"Your status is safe with me," he said in a tone that produced the desired result of making her laugh.

It had been so long since she'd laughed at anything but the antics of her toddlers. "I overreacted," she admitted. "Force of habit." She figured she didn't need to explain to him that at this point her life consisted of one spiral of exhaustion after another. It would be the height of foolishness not to want a night off, especially if it meant spending an evening alone with Callum.

"I don't have any babysitters I trust," she said honestly. "I guess I could ask one of the women from the pediatric center day care. The girls adore them." The waitress returned with Callum's card. He signed the slip and they both stood. "Would you like me to take Sasha?" she offered.

"I've got her," he said, snagging the diaper bag from the table and slinging it over his empty arm.

"Thank you," she said.

He gave her a slow half smile that she felt all the way to her toes. For a moment it was difficult to remember they were in a public place, each of them holding one of her daughters. The urge to lean in and brush her lips across his was almost too much to resist.

His grin widened as if he could read her mind and liked the path of her thoughts.

She spun on her heel and hurried out of the restaurant.

"You move quick for a woman holding a baby," he said lightly when they were on the sidewalk.

"I can do almost anything holding a baby." She cringed at how strange the comment sounded. "I mean—"

"I remember that from when my sisters were babies." He fell in step beside her as she started toward her car. "Stephanie was four when the triplets were born. All three of them loved being carried. We used to joke that for the first two years of their lives, their feet never touched the floor."

"My upper body is super strong," she said with a smile. "Although they're getting big enough that I won't be able to carry them both at the same time for long. Someone is going to have to learn to like walking since they're stuck with just me."

"They aren't stuck," Callum reminded her gently.

They'd reached the minivan. Becky hit a button on the key fob, and the side door slid open. She strapped the girls into their car seats, and the two of them immediately began babbling softly to each other.

"Spending time with you makes me feel like the lamest person in the world," she told Callum as she straightened from the car.

He blew out a disbelieving laugh. "I make you feel lame?"

"That didn't come out right." She pressed two fingers to her chest as her heart beat at a manic pace. "You make me realize how small my life is at the moment."

"Small and lame." He raised a brow. "The hits just keep on coming."

She shook her head as she pressed the button inside the car to close the side door. How could she explain the tumult of emotions racing through her? "We've had dinner twice now."

"Enjoyable both times," he said quickly.

"The first time, you had to hear about my late husband." She flicked a glance toward the car. "Tonight we covered all my insecurities about motherhood. Not exactly scintillating conversation on either count."

"It is to me." He took her hand and drew her forward a few steps so that they were standing a few paces away from the car door, out of the line of sight of the twins in their car seats. "I can't quite explain it, but everything about you fascinates me."

She laughed. "This isn't selling myself short, but

I might be the least fascinating person in Rambling Rose."

"You are brave, strong, independent, determined, loyal, loving."

"You make me sound better than I am." His words rolled around her brain, searching for a place to fit. She'd always thought of herself as a survivalist. She did what she needed to in the moment. Could she actually see herself the way Callum did? She loved the idea of it.

"That is who you are."

His voice rumbled over her, and she realized she'd swayed closer to him, lured by the promise of someone seeing her in the way Callum did.

The longing to kiss him that she'd felt in the restaurant pulsed through her again. Even in the dim glow of the streetlight, she could see the gold flecks in his dark eyes. They'd appeared solid brown at first glance but they were more distinct than that. Much like Callum, the nearer she got the more detail she could appreciate. There were so many facets to this man underneath the polished facade. She wanted to know them all.

She felt the hitch in his breath and then his mouth brushed over hers, light as a touch of a butterfly's wings. Awareness zinged along her skin like his touch was electric. Or maybe it was the energy inside her that had been waiting to be set free.

When he would have pulled back, Becky leaned in, unwilling to let the moment go so soon. Her enthusiasm was rewarded by Callum's soft groan of pleasure. He fitted his mouth to hers more thoroughly and his fingers gripped the back of her shirt like he was trying to root them both in place. Desire raced through her, a cresting wave she wanted to ride forever.

As lost as she was in his embrace, a soft squeak from inside the car had her jerking away. She peered in the window to see Luna and Sasha holding hands. It wasn't clear which one of them had made the noise, but they appeared content for the moment.

"I should go," she whispered, pressing her fingers to her kiss-swollen lips. It was a wonder she didn't feel a sizzle even now, like a drop of water on a hot pan. "The girls need to get to sleep. Thanks again for dinner."

"It was the highlight of my week," Callum said.

"Me, too," she told him, hoping her knees didn't give out. She didn't want the night to end but climbed into her car as Callum watched, her heart full and her body alive in the most intoxicating way.

Chapter Six

The next morning, Callum found his sister unloading supplies into a storage closet at the vet clinic. "Can you do me a favor?" he asked.

Stephanie looked over her shoulder. "As long as it doesn't involve patching the drywall or installing flooring in the front lobby."

"No manual labor," he confirmed. "I need you to babysit."

She turned. "That's cute, Callum, but you're a big boy now. I'll make you a snack, but I don't think you need a babysitter."

"Funny, Steph." He massaged a hand over the back of his neck. Asking for help of any kind didn't come easy to him. But he needed this. "Would you babysit Becky's twins for a night?"

His sister's eyes lit up. "Are you serious? I'd love to get my hands on those babies."

"Maybe take the enthusiasm down a notch. You sound a little scary right now."

"Do you want my help or not?" She gave him a playful nudge. "Those twins are adorable. I'm not scary, but I'm surprised Becky is willing to leave them for an evening. Obviously they go to day care, but she seems like the type of mom who'd have trouble taking any time for herself."

He sighed. "That's why I need your help," he admitted. "Luna and Sasha are adorable and sweet, but I'd like to treat Becky to a night out. She's worried about leaving them with a sitter."

"It's understandable," Stephanie said, her tone turning wistful in a way he didn't understand. "Being a mother is a big responsibility, especially on your own."

Callum studied his sister, trying to figure out where this contemplative mood had come from. He'd been in the role of big brother for so long that sometimes he forgot his younger sisters were adults with aspects of their lives he knew nothing about. "You'll find someone," he told her gently.

"I'm not looking for a man," she said, almost defiantly. "I don't need to fall in love to have a full life."

He held up his hands, palms out. "I understand that. I'm just saying I want to see you happy."

"Goes both ways. Becky makes you happy, doesn't she?"

How could he put into words all the things Becky made him feel? Excited. Nervous. Distracted. Enamored. Beside himself with desire. "We're friends," he said simply.

"Just because your marriage ended the way it did doesn't mean you're trash at relationships."

Callum chuckled. Leave it to Stephanie to cut right to the heart of his issue. Yes, he had a feeling he was garbage at commitment, to say the least. Too much responsibility on his shoulders so young in life had left him with a fierce streak of independence. He didn't like to be tied down by anything except his work because that was the only piece of his life he could truly control.

"I appreciate the vote of confidence."

"It's true."

"Maybe. But who knows how long I'll stay in Rambling Rose? All of our projects are on schedule. Once everything is up and running, it might be time for me to move on. I've been looking at a couple of locations around Texas—communities with potential."

"What about the potential for you to stick around?" Stephanie grabbed another box of supplies. "You can't keep hopping from one location to the next. We all need roots."

Sometimes those roots can feel like they're choking you, Callum thought, although he wouldn't say the words out loud. The topic of his role in the family and how that had impacted the man he'd become was a sensitive one.

He never wanted his sisters to feel as if he resented the role he'd played in their lives but he couldn't deny its effect on him.

"I'm happy with the life I have," he said, earning an eye roll from Stephanie.

"One of these days you're going to want more," she told him as if she were far older and wiser than her twenty-seven years. "For now, let's leave it that I'd be happy to babysit for Becky's girls. Most of my evenings are free so just let me know what night."

"Thanks." He pulled her close for a quick hug. "Steven texted that the new order of cabinets is almost ready. That should keep things on schedule."

"I never doubted either of you," she said.

After checking in with the on-site foreman, Callum drove over to the future site of The Shoppes at Rambling Rose, which was scheduled to open after the veterinary clinic, and then checked out progress at the spa. He thought about what could happen if he decided to make Rambling Rose his permanent home. His stomach pitched in response. A benefit to keeping his connections to the communities where he worked casual was he had no fear of being forced to put down roots or disappointing anyone when he couldn't. He was like a revitalization fairy godfather, swooping in to make changes, then moving on to the next big thing before anyone expected too much of him.

Callum wasn't sure if he had the capacity to change who he was now, even if he tried.

"Thank you so much for agreeing to stay with them." Becky offered Callum's sister a grateful smile. "They can be a handful."

"I'm used to multiple energy thanks to the triplets," Stephanie answered. Her shiny hair was pulled back into a loose bun and she wore a casual sweater and faded jeans, the epitome of effortless beauty. "And I love babies at this age." She grinned as Sasha started a game of peekaboo. Never wanting to relinquish the spotlight to her sister, Luna also began hiding her face behind her blanket, then popping back out. "The three of us are going to have a great evening." She met Becky's gaze, understanding darkening her blue eyes. "Don't worry. I'll text with updates and call if we need anything."

Becky gave a jerky nod. "I left instructions on the counter."

"We should go." Callum put a gentle hand on her elbow. "I'm not sure they'll hold the reservation if we're late."

Nervous energy fluttering in her chest, Becky kissed both girls goodbye. Often one or the other of them made a fuss when she tried to walk out of the day care center in the morning, but tonight they seemed more than ready to stay with Stephanie.

"Your sister is really good with kids," she told Callum as she shut the door behind them. Tonight he wore dark slacks and a white button-down shirt that seemed to accentuate his tanned complexion. His hair skimmed the collar, and the top button of the shirt was open. Becky had the almost uncontrollable urge to kiss that soft spot at the base of his neck.

"She was excited to babysit," he confirmed.

Becky scanned the street in front of her house. "Where's your truck?"

He grinned. "I thought we could take something a little sportier tonight since we don't have car seats to contend with."

He pointed to a sleek, two-seater Audi parked at the curb.

"How did I not notice that car?" Becky stifled a giggle. "It's so out of place in this neighborhood." She tugged on the sleeve of the dress she'd chosen for the evening, a floral-patterned wrap dress that just skimmed her knees.

Although she'd had it for a few years, she hadn't had

the opportunity to wear it since before her pregnancy. Slipping into it tonight, she was shocked to discover that it fit her differently from how it used to. She thought she'd lost her pregnancy weight, but the dress clung to her breasts and hips more tightly than she remembered. "Is this too casual for where we're going?"

"You look beautiful," he said as he took her hand. "Your skin is like ivory satin."

"Callum Fortune, are you a secret poet?" she asked with a grin.

"Just trying to live up to my reputation as a Renaissance man." He opened the door of the Audi for her, and she slid into the passenger side, unable to resist running her palm across the car's leather interior.

She'd never been in such a luxurious vehicle, and the reminder of how different their lives were had anxiety flitting through her like caffeine pumping in her veins.

"It's just a car," Callum said as he got in next to her. "It doesn't mean anything."

She barked out a laugh, then rolled her eyes at him. "Only a person who could afford a car like this would think that. You're rich."

He pulled away from the curb, shooting her a genuinely confused glance. "Is that a bad thing?"

"Would you believe I've never known any really rich people?" She scrunched up her nose. "Doctors around here make a good living, but not like your family."

"The car was a stupid idea," he muttered, and she instantly felt guilty.

"No. Of course not." She shook her head. "The car is fun." She placed a hand on his arm. "I just want you to understand that you don't need to try to impress me with your money or your connections or anything material. I like you, Callum. Who you are as a person means more than anything else. Even if you drove some kind of a beater car and didn't live in a huge mansion in a gated community, I'd want to spend time with you. I like you because of you."

They'd stopped at a red light just before turning onto the highway that led out of town. Callum looked toward her with so much intensity in his gaze, heat flamed her cheeks. "You're staring," she told him softly.

"You calling me out as a rich boy might have been the nicest thing anyone has ever said to me." He leaned over the console and quickly kissed her before the light turned green.

She laughed. "I meant it as a compliment. I know you work hard, and I'm not judging you for having money. But it isn't why I like you."

"I'm glad."

She blew out a breath and settled back against the seat as he drove. She was glad he hadn't been offended by what she'd told him. Saying the words out loud made her relax in a way she hadn't expected. There wasn't a true explanation for why the disparities in their backgrounds affected her. Becky had a feeling she was looking for any excuse as to why things couldn't work out between them.

She was falling for Callum, which gave him the power to hurt her. She normally kept her emotions on lockdown for the sake of her girls. There were certain things she didn't allow herself to feel—pity or regret for the life she'd lost when Rick died or bitterness at having to manage all the things on her own. Callum made her want to throw the shackles off her heart and claim a second chance at love.

Biting down on the inside of her cheek, Becky reminded herself that this couldn't be love. She'd known the man for just a week. He was handsome and kind. End of story. At least for her.

"This is why Rambling Rose needs more dining options," Callum said as the sun dipped below the horizon. "I don't want to have to drive almost an hour to take my girl out on a date."

His girl. Warmth bloomed inside her at the thought of being claimed by Callum. Could she trust what was happening between them? Was she even on the right page about it?

"A more upscale restaurant would be a nice addition to the community," she agreed. "Probably some of the people who live out by you would like that better."

He threw her a sidelong glance. "You make it sound as if we're the Texas version of *Downton Abbey*."

She groaned. "Do I sound like I have a chip on my shoulders? I don't mean to. My parents always made it really clear that I should know my place, so I guess that advice stuck."

"Know your place," he murmured. "What does that mean exactly?"

"Not to reach for things above my station."

"Seriously?"

"They meant it in a helpful way." She shook her head. "I think. When I say it out loud, it sounds terrible. I'd never want my girls to believe they shouldn't try for the moon. Whatever they want to accomplish, I'll support them, even if they fail."

"Everyone fails at something," Callum said, and his voice held a note of regret she didn't understand.

"What is your biggest failure?" she asked, curiosity and trepidation warring inside her.

His knuckles turned white as his fingers tightened on the steering wheel. He was silent so long Becky thought he might not answer. "Marriage," he said finally.

Becky tried to hide her gasp. "You were married?"

"And divorced after a year," he continued.

"What happened?" she blurted before thinking about it. Maybe he didn't want to share that part of himself with her. They'd had two dinners and a handful of lunches together and he hadn't mentioned having an ex-wife.

"I was a terrible husband." He pulled into the parking lot of a fancy-looking restaurant housed in a historic mansion on the outskirts of Austin.

"Callum."

He turned off the car, then faced her, regret shining in his eyes. "I shouldn't have brought this up tonight, Becky. I'm sorry. I've been wanting to tell you but now isn't the right time."

She reached for his hand. "I've talked to you about far too many details of my life. I'm glad you shared that bit of yourself with me. If it makes you uncomfortable, I understand. But I want to hear about it. I want to know you."

Lifting her hand to his mouth, he brushed a gentle kiss across her knuckles. "You really are amazing."

"Hardly." She laughed and dropped her gaze to her lap.

"Let's get our table and have a drink." He gave her a pleading look. "Then I promise I'll tell you anything you want to know about my past."

She tried not to let nerves settle over her as they entered the restaurant. It had a modern farmhouse vibe but still held true to the era of the house with rich textures and beautiful artwork. A stone fireplace dominated the far wall, and she wondered if she'd ever been in such a gorgeous establishment.

"What made you choose this place?" she asked as they approached the hostess's stand.

He shrugged. "It's been written up in several regional papers to rave reviews. Apparently, people come from all over to eat here. When I think about opening an upscale restaurant in Rambling Rose, I want to know what is already working in the area."

The hostess took his name and led them to a cozy table near the fireplace.

"So it's a date *and* a research trip?" Becky asked with a wink.

"Ninety-nine percent date," he assured her.

The waiter, an older gentleman with a shock of white hair, brought each of them a menu and explained the evening's specials, which included a scallop sashimi appetizer and Kobe beef tenderloin medallions with braised leeks for a main course. Becky was certain she'd never eaten anything as fancy as the dishes he described.

Callum ordered a bottle of wine, and she saw the waiter's eyes widen a fraction. When he left, she leaned in over the table. "What's so special about the wine you ordered?"

His thick brows drew together. "Nothing really. It's simply a good vintage."

"Does that translate as pricey?"

"Will you let me spoil you tonight?" he asked softly,

reaching across the table to lace their fingers together. "Please?"

The *please* got her.

"If you insist. We'll enjoy this evening and you can make me feel like a princess." She leaned closer to him. "Although I'll let you in on a little secret in case you haven't picked up on it. I always feel special with you."

His chest rose and fell as if her words made it difficult for him to catch his breath. She liked the idea of affecting him in that way. She didn't want to be the only one caught up in the spell of whatever was happening between them.

Chapter Seven

Callum was grateful that the wine steward approached their table at that moment. He'd been half tempted to tug Becky right out of her seat and into his lap. Or better yet to skip dinner altogether and find a nearby hotel where he could spend the next several hours making her feel special from head to toe.

The sommelier held up the bottle for his inspection and, at Callum's subtle nod, began to uncork it while praising the vintage and offering bland small talk about the wine industry. Callum was used to this routine in the restaurants he frequented, especially after ordering a five-hundred-dollar bottle. Of course, he wouldn't share the price with Becky. Part of him worried she'd be too nervous to actually take a drink if she knew how much it cost.

He hadn't been lying when he told her he wanted to

treat her this evening. If he'd been more on the ball, he would have chartered a helicopter and flown them to Houston or Dallas for a true five-star meal. Next time—if she gave him a next time.

As he took the cork from the sommelier, Callum felt a light pressure on his leg. He went to take the requisite sniff and ended up almost shoving the cork up his own nose when he realized it was Becky playing an innocent game of footsy with him under the table. Every nerve ending tensed and it took a herculean amount of effort to keep his features neutral.

One corner of her mouth curved up into a mischievous smile, but she kept her gaze trained on the wine steward.

"Perhaps the lovely lady would like a taste," Callum suggested as he handed the cork back to the man.

With an agreeable nod, the sommelier poured a finger of the deep burgundy liquid into a glass and gave it to Becky. She didn't bother to swirl the glass, and Callum noticed the man's mouth furrow into a disapproving scowl.

Instead, she took a dainty sip. "Tastes like red wine," she reported after a moment.

There was an indignant mew of distress from the sommelier. "It's not just ordinary wine," he explained, and Callum could tell the man was doing his best not to sound horrified. "That is a perfectly balanced vintage that's both bold and complex. It's like a symphony in your mouth."

"Which is a complicated way of saying 'great red wine,'" Callum explained, earning a slightly wider smile from Becky. What would it take to coax a full-fledged grin from her?

He desperately wanted to know.

"It's lovely," she told the sommelier, taking pity on the wine expert's obvious distress.

"I'm glad you're enjoying it," the man answered as he poured more wine into her glass. He filled Callum's glass as well and then left the table. The waiter returned to take their dinner orders, and then they were blessedly alone. Or as alone as they could be in a quiet corner of the restaurant.

"You distracted me," Callum accused playfully.

Becky held up her wineglass. "To distractions."

"You can distract me anytime," he told her as they clinked glasses, then frowned as he took a sip. "I'm missing something."

"What's that?"

"Your foot under the table."

She giggled, then flashed the exuberant grin he'd been waiting for all night. "I should probably apologize, except I'm not sorry. That man was far too serious for his own good."

"But you like the wine?"

"I understand very little about what makes it so special, but even I can tell that it is."

Callum opened his mouth to reply, then shut it again. He felt the exact same way about Becky. Yes, she was beautiful. He'd dated beautiful women before. Women who were ambitious and accomplished. But he couldn't remember ever having been so affected by any of them.

"Do you still want to know about my past?" he asked almost reluctantly.

"Of course."

He gave a gruff nod and took another drink. As much as he didn't want to speak about it, he knew they couldn't go further unless she understood his shortcomings. He liked and respected Becky, and was crazy attracted to her, but none of those things changed who he was on the inside. What he could and couldn't offer her. Best to have it all out now so she wouldn't hope for more.

"Doralee and I met at a bar in Nashville. It was a fast courtship, and we married within a couple of months."

"Like Rick and me," she murmured.

He hadn't realized the similarity in the time frame of their previous marriages. "I'm not sure I'd compare the two. I thought we were on the same page as far as the paths we wanted our lives to travel. Turns out we weren't even reading from the same playbook." He shook his head. "My business was starting to take off, and I had people coming to me about real estate deals in several smaller towns throughout Tennessee and the surrounding area. Steven and Dillon had joined me at that point, and I spent a lot of time working."

"You're dedicated."

"I should have been more dedicated to my marriage," he admitted, shifting in his seat. "She resented everything about Fortune Brothers Construction. In turn, I felt restricted, like she wanted to control me. The whole thing was a mess, and the entirety of it was my fault."

Becky inclined her head as she studied him, her gaze gentle. If she argued with him or offered false platitudes to assuage his guilt, Callum might lose his mind. He couldn't go back and fix the pain he'd caused his ex-wife, so the regret he carried with him like his own version of Sisyphus's boulder was all he had.

"Do you ever speak to her?" Becky asked, one slender finger circling the rim of her glass.

The breath he hadn't realized he was holding escaped his lips on a sudden hiss. "She called me this week, actually." Something flashed in Becky's dark eyes. He couldn't name the emotion, but it warmed him just the same.

"Just to catch up?" she asked, a little too evenly.

"To tell me she's engaged." He drained the rest of his wine, then waived away the server who moved to refill his glass. "She's been dating a guy since shortly after our divorce was finalized."

"How does that make you feel?"

"Like more of a failure than I already did."

"Callum, no."

"I'm joking." He gave what he hoped was a convincing laugh. "Sort of. I'm happy for her. She deserves a good man and a great life. I wish I could have been the one to give it to her. I'm sorry she had to go through our wreck of a marriage to find her happily-ever-after or whatever you want to call it."

"Sometimes it takes going through a difficult period to truly appreciate the happiness on the other side."

They were pretty words, but he didn't know if he could allow himself to trust them.

"Do you really believe that?"

The smile she gave him was filled with yearning. "I have to."

Right. Because this woman had been through something so much worse than the breakdown of a marriage.

Their food arrived, and he loved the way her eyes lit up at the sight of the mouthwatering dish the server set on the table in front of her. Becky had ordered some complicated chicken dish while he got steak.

She moaned in pleasure after her first bite. "I might

not know a lot about fancy wine, but this is the most amazing dinner I've ever had." She pointed her fork at Callum. "You should definitely take notes on this restaurant and recreate its goodness in Rambling Rose. Steal away the chef if you have to. I'll spend a month eating peanut butter sandwiches for every meal just to save money to go out to a place like this."

He wanted to assure her that she didn't have to worry about money because he'd take care of her, but he couldn't make that promise. Even if he could commit to it, he had a feeling he'd just offend her by offering. Even if they didn't say so out loud, most of the women Callum dated liked his wealth. The fact that Becky made a point of being genuinely not impressed felt refreshing.

"That's a ringing endorsement."

She nodded around another bite, then lifted up her hand to obstruct his view of her face. "Sorry," she said after a moment. "Eating quickly is a habit with me now. I can't remember the last time I ate at a leisurely pace."

"Have more wine," he suggested.

She flashed him a look of mock horror. "Are you trying to get me tipsy?"

"Not at all," he answered without hesitation. "But I do plan to kiss you tonight. A lot. And I want no question in either of our minds that we're both willing participants."

"I'm willing," she whispered, her eyes sparkling.

He smothered a groan. "When you look at me that way I want to skip dessert and ask for the check right now."

"When we're together," she said, leaning closer, "you make me want to be the dessert."

Color flooded her cheeks as she made the flirty statement, but the effect on him was the same as if she'd been a seasoned seductress.

As perfectly prepared as the meal was, Callum barely tasted it. He couldn't wait to be alone with Becky, even for a few moments.

"I'm so embarrassed," she murmured. "I don't say things like that."

"Then I'm not sure whether I'm more honored or turned on," he told her with a laugh.

They finished eating, the air around them charged with an electric current of desire. She left the table to call and check in with Stephanie as he paid the check. He found her just outside the restaurant's entrance, staring up at a clear night sky filled with stars.

"Everything okay?" he asked as he moved toward her.

"Yes," she reported with a relieved sigh. "Your sister said the girls went to bed without a fuss and have been sleeping soundly ever since." She dipped her chin, looking up at him through her lashes, and added, "She said to take our time."

"I intend to," he said, his voice rough even to his own ears. He took her hand and led her around the side of the building, then turned his back to the cool brick, drawing her closer. Need rushed through him as their lips met, and there was no holding back the flood of desire. She seemed as frenzied as he felt, opening for him as soon as he drew his tongue across the seam of her lips. The kiss deepened, need exploding through him like a wildfire.

Her body formed to his, soft where his was hard, and he spread his hands across her back, wanting more from her than she could possibly give out in the open, even sheltered as they were by the darkness and shadows.

He forced himself to bank his yearning, to slow the pace to where he could savor her. They kissed until he couldn't tell where he left off and she began. The flare of desire almost overwhelmed him with its intensity, his body hot and ready.

She broke away from the embrace when a horn sounded in a parking lot, glancing around in shock before offering a tentative smile. "I was afraid we were going to get caught making out like teenagers."

"Wouldn't have been the worst thing that's happened."

"But mortifying just the same." She straightened her dress. "I'm a mother of twins. Moms don't kiss like that."

He reached out and cupped her jaw, unable to stop himself from touching her. "Who told you that?"

She arched a brow. "Chapter three in *The New Mom Handbook*."

"There's a handbook?"

"I'm joking." She leaned into his touch, like a cat begging to be petted. He flicked the tip of her earlobe with his thumb, and she bit down on her lip. "We should go. I don't want to take advantage of your sister's generosity."

He wasn't ready for the night to end, but didn't want to push too far. This had been a big step for Becky, trusting her daughters with a babysitter and allowing herself a rare evening out.

"I've had the best time," he said as he took her hand.

"You really spoiled me," she told him. "I almost feel like a princess."

There was so much more he wanted to give her, to show her. If only she'd let him.

The thought pinged through his brain that maybe he should pump the brakes on their connection. Hell, he couldn't even commit to the restaurant idea, as strong as it was, because that would mean more time in Rambling Rose. His original plan had been to move on after the last of his initial slate of projects opened. That was his sweet spot as far as staying in one place. Enough time to make a difference in the community but not so long that he'd be tempted to stay.

Becky was a temptation he hadn't expected, and he had no clue what to do about it.

The next week was a blur for Becky. The pediatric center continued to be busy, and her days sped by in a whir of patient care and paperwork. Of course, that didn't count the moments she spent fantasizing about Callum.

She couldn't deny that her feelings had intensified since their special evening out. He was so much more than she'd expected him to be. Handsome as sin was hard enough to resist. Callum was the whole package— smart, successful, generous and kind.

As great as the fancy restaurant had been, she had just as much fun with him on casual nights at her house. He came over almost every evening after she got off work. They took turns grocery shopping and would cook together while the twins watched from the high chairs or played nearby. She would have thought he'd get bored with her daily routine, but he didn't seem to mind the monotony of life with toddlers.

After the girls went to bed, Becky and Callum would

spend hours each evening talking and then even more time kissing. She came alive in his embrace. It became more difficult each night to let him go. He seemed as reluctant to leave her as she was to watch him drive away through the flutter of curtains at her front window.

Which was how she found herself on an ordinary Tuesday night, standing in the open doorway of her small house trying to force her arms to unwind from around Callum's broad shoulders.

"I have to go," he said, then claimed her mouth with his.

"It's late," she agreed when they finally came up for air. "You should go."

It took another several minutes before she finally lowered her hands to her sides and backed up a step.

"I had an amazing time," he told her.

"We ate spaghetti with sauce from a jar and watched reruns," she pointed out with a laugh.

"It doesn't matter." He dropped a kiss on the tip of her nose. "With you, it's always amazing."

Stay, she wanted to tell him. Surely he would understand what that one word meant. She wanted more from Callum. As much as he could give her.

Right now she simply wanted him to stay.

But she didn't speak the word out loud.

Instead, she watched as he shoved his hands into the pockets of his jeans and backed away down her front walk.

"Good night, Becky," he called and then turned and jogged to his car. Almost as if he couldn't wait to get away.

She hoped he was moving quickly so that he wouldn't turn around and invite himself back into her house.

She slammed the front door shut like she might chase him down the street without the barrier between them. She moved to the window because it hurt her heart—not to mention the rest of her body—to know he was driving away. His taillights glowed red against the midnight darkness as he pulled away from the curb.

He'd driven only a few feet when his brake lights went on. Becky's breath hitched as the truck reversed back into its former spot against the curb in front of her house. For several long minutes nothing happened. No movement. No lights. No Callum.

Then the truck's interior lit up for a few seconds as he climbed out of the cab. He walked around the front of the vehicle and up her walk. Back to her house. To her.

Becky didn't give fear or doubt a chance to take hold in her brain. She dropped the curtain and rushed to the front door, throwing it open and dashing toward Callum. He grinned as she hurtled herself into his arms.

"I want you to stay," she whispered into his ear.

"Exactly what I hoped you'd say," he said as he carried her into the house.

Chapter Eight

As soon as Callum kicked the door shut behind them, Becky's doubts returned in full force. She wanted him more than she could have imagined, but her husband was the only man she'd ever been with in that way. And while she wasn't anywhere near over the hill, motherhood had changed her body.

She also had to deal with the issue of how much of her heart she could to give Callum. For her, sex meant more than just the physical act. Although she had no doubt he would be attentive and thoughtful, what if for him it was just a release? Scratching an itch between two people untethered to anyone else.

"Does it hurt?" he asked as he took a step away from her.

She blinked. "What?"

His mouth curved into that sexy hint of a smile that

never failed to drive her crazy. "You look like you're thinking way too hard. Typically, my brain hurts when I try that."

"You should *try* being less perceptive," she told him with an eye roll. "It's kind of annoying."

He chuckled, the low sound rippling across her already taut nerve endings. "Nothing has to happen tonight, Becky. You're in control."

Her breath caught in her throat. When was the last time she'd felt truly in control? Before tragedy had turned her into a widow and a single mother of two unborn babies. Since that moment, she'd been furiously treading water with the waves constantly lapping over her head.

"We can talk," he continued. "You can tell me to go."

"But I told you to stay," she reminded him.

He tucked a loose strand of hair behind her ear. "You're allowed to change your mind."

"I haven't," she blurted. "I'm just nervous. It's been a while and…" She shook her head.

"And…"

"Carrying twins pretty much wrecked my body," she said on a long exhale.

It was now, apparently, Callum's turn to blink. Poor guy. She had no doubt any man would struggle with a good response to that kind of statement. It had been stupid to put the silly doubt into words but…

"You're beautiful," he told her gently. His finger traced a path from the side of her jaw down her throat and along the edge of the neckline of the dress she wore. "Sometimes when you blush, it flushes all the way to your chest. I'm dying to know if I can make your whole body blush."

Her mouth went dry.

"I love how you're soft in all the places where I'm hard." He stepped closer, his warmth heating her like a fire on a cold winter night. "It's as if you're formed in the exact right way to fit me. If this is too soon, we don't have to—"

"I want to," she admitted, unable to offer any other response. She knew she had to stay in the moment. She had a feeling this was uncharted territory for both of them.

"Are you sure?" he asked, and she appreciated that he was giving her so many chances to decide. The feeling of being in control was a revelation in her current life where every day she felt strapped into an exhilarating and exhausting roller coaster with no safety harness.

She took his hand and led him through the quiet house to her bedroom. It had been the one space she'd changed after her husband's death, when sorrow had been her late-night companion. She'd thought her grief might engulf her, even knowing she carried a legacy of love inside her. Then she'd felt the first flutter of movement. A quiver of butterfly wings signaling the lives growing in her belly. At that moment she'd understood that she needed to make peace with her sorrow and try to find some measure of happiness again. For her babies.

She'd cleaned out the room, not just of Rick's belongings, but everything. She'd spent a portion of her meager savings to buy new furniture and hired a local handyman to repaint the walls from nondescript beige to a soft yellow. The color felt like hope, and now she realized she had been preparing for this new chapter in her life without even realizing it.

Moonlight slanted through the window, alighting on Callum's strong features. Slowly, she stepped closer and wound her arms around his neck. She didn't move deliberately because of fear. Somehow his allowing her to choose had chased away her doubts, at least for the moment. Instead, she wanted to enjoy each second they had together. Unwrap this experience like a precious gift.

He kissed her like he felt the same, molding his lips to hers until soft sounds of aching hunger escaped her throat. His hands moved along her back, over the dress's fine fabric, sending shivers along her skin. As good as his touch felt, it wasn't enough. She broke the kiss and began to unbutton his shirt, her fingers shaky with need.

"Let me," he told her as he took over. Within seconds he'd made quick work of the buttons and was shrugging out of the crisp fabric.

Becky did her best not to whimper. It had been no secret that Callum had an amazing body, his muscular physique evident even under his clothes. His bare chest and perfectly toned muscles made her forget her own name.

"Do you go to a tanning bed?" she asked, taking in all that golden skin and needing to regain some self-control.

He chuckled. "Uh, never."

She put her hands on her hips. "I just can't get over how naturally bronze you are."

"Do you want me to prove I have no tan lines?" He winked as he unhooked his belt.

"Yes, please," she whispered, and he laughed again.

"I think you need to catch up," he told her. "I'm feeling slightly underdressed at the moment."

"Don't let it bother you," she assured him. "It's working for me."

He arched a brow in response.

She hitched up the hem of her dress. The soft fabric pulled on over her head, no zipper or buttons to fuss with. But it also meant that in the disrobing, she'd bare her body to him without being able to see his split-second initial reaction. Becky couldn't decide if that was a blessing or a curse.

"Here goes everything," she whispered and lifted the dress up and off in one fluid movement. It fell to the floor in a whisper of sound, leaving her standing in front of Callum in her bra and panties. She didn't even own a matching set since motherhood had changed her breasts.

He didn't seem to mind. A shiver rippled through him as he stared at her. Her heart leaped in her chest at the intensity in his brown eyes.

His throat bobbed as he swallowed. "You take my breath away."

Confidence building in step with the desire pooling low in her belly, she reached behind her back and flicked open her bra. The straps dropped from her shoulders and then the lace fell to the floor.

Callum muttered a strained curse, his eyes going darker than she thought possible.

He closed the distance between them in two quick steps, claiming her mouth for a rough and ravishing kiss. She met his need with her own, thrilled when his big hands cradled her breasts, thumbs skimming over the sensitive peaks of her nipples.

Just as her knees gave way, he caught her and moved toward the bed, yanking back the covers and lowering her gently onto the sheets. They continued to kiss as he explored her body. It felt as if he was trying to memorize every curve and dip. She barely recognized herself in the way she responded, her desire greedy and sharp.

Becky was at her heart a people pleaser, always wanting to accommodate others without taking anything for herself. So the soft demands she spoke startled her, but Callum had no problem following every one. It was clear he wanted to learn how she liked to be touched. In the process, his inventive hands and mouth offered new insight into pleasure.

He was both gentle and demanding as he explored her. She easily opened for him as his fingers skimmed below the waistband of her panties, delving into her hot center in a way that made her arch into him. Blood roared in her ears, and pressure built inside her, more intense than she'd ever experienced. Her skin fairly crackled with the pleasure of the way he touched her.

She cried out his name when her release roared through her with all the force of a cannonball. Callum whispered sweet words into her ear as her body recovered, but still she wanted more.

"I need you," she said against his skin, delighted by the subtle tremor that threaded through him.

"The best three words I've ever heard." He kissed her swiftly, then climbed off the bed and reached for his discarded pants. He took a condom packet from the wallet, then turned to face her. Anticipation flooded her once again as he shucked out of his boxers, appearing not self-conscious in the least about standing naked in front of her.

Why should he? His body was perfection. He

sheathed himself as he returned to the bed, his weight giving her a feeling of safety.

"Every night," she said, leaning up to kiss the base of his throat, "I've watched you drive away, and a part of me has wanted to call you back."

He settled between her legs but didn't move to enter her. "Which part?"

"All of them, really." She offered a slow smile. "All of me."

With his elbows resting on either side of her, he cradled her face in his hands. "Those are the parts I want," he confirmed. "All of you."

"I'm yours," she whispered as he filled her in one sure thrust.

She'd been made for this moment, and it was everything and more. Her fingers trailed along the muscles of his shoulders and back, reveling in his strength and power. He continued to rain kisses along her face as they found a rhythm unique to the two of them. Time seemed to stand still as they remained suspended in this moment.

Her nerve endings shuddered when the pressure built again, different from what had happened to her minutes earlier. This time she and Callum climbed the high peak together, and then suddenly fireworks exploded throughout her body. She felt Callum go taut and he said her name like it was the most beautiful word he'd ever spoken.

"Amazing," he said into her hair moments later, dropping kisses like feathers on the top of her head.

She didn't know how to respond, what to say to explain how much this moment meant to her. She couldn't even admit it to herself, because she knew she loved this man. Not just because of great sex, although that was a bonus. She'd fallen for him for so many reasons, and being with him in this way had only served to crash through the last of her defenses.

Instead, she kissed him again, hoping to convey what she wanted him to know without giving away too much of herself. She let out a little groan of protest when he left her to go to the bathroom, only to return a few minutes later and gather her close.

"I'll be gone before morning," he promised, the comfort of his warm body making her blissfully drowsy. "But let me hold you awhile longer."

As an answer, she snuggled closer, falling asleep with his arms around her.

"Please don't say you're going to try to become a farmer now, too?"

Callum turned with a grin as Dillon and Steven walked into the abandoned feed house situated two blocks off the main drag of Rambling Rose's downtown.

He held out his hands, palms up. "Not exactly, although right now I don't think there's anything Fortune Brothers Construction can't accomplish in this town."

Dillon shook his head, a lock of sandy-blond hair falling across his forehead. "You shouldn't say that to anyone," his younger brother warned. "I've already heard rumblings about the locals not liking how much property we've bought in town. People think we're catering to the new millionaires—the gated community crowd."

"Not true," Steven argued before Callum could speak. "The pediatric center serves everyone, as will the vet clinic."

"What about the spa and the upscale shopping center and hotel?" Dillon kicked a toe at the dirty concrete floor. "Those aren't exactly meant for the average resident."

Callum stepped forward. "But they'll generate revenue and tax dollars that will help the town." He put a hand on Dillon's muscled shoulder. Dillon had always been the peacemaker of the family and the worrier within their business partnership, his cautious nature balancing the ambition that Callum and Steven shared.

"So if you aren't reopening the feed store," Dillon said, spinning in a slow circle to take in the dilapidated space, "why are we here?"

"Because I wanted the two of you to be the first to see the site of our next project."

Both of his brothers blinked.

"We're developing an upscale restaurant," he explained.

"In a feed store?" Dillon barked out a laugh. "I like the irony. Feed store as a restaurant, although it doesn't actually lend itself to upscale."

"You just need to see the vision," Callum assured his brother. He walked a few paces away from them and pointed to an open stretch of wall. "Imagine a long bar there, serving hand-mixed cocktails." He gestured to the far side of the space. "A kitchen with state-of-the-art equipment. We'll source local and regional ingredients along with the craft beer and liquor."

"My mouth is watering already," Steven said.

Dillon shook his head. "Do I need to point out that none of us has experience running a restaurant? We're contractors."

"But Ashley, Megan and Nicole do," Callum reminded him. "I talked to the three of them last night and they are interested in investing and heading up the design and menu."

"They want to come to Rambling Rose to run a restaurant?" Dillon scratched his chin.

"Their own restaurant," Callum clarified.

"The triplets are a force of nature." Steven shook his head. "You realize that, right?"

Callum smiled. "We've got plenty of room at Fame and Fortune." It might drive him crazy sometimes to balance all the intricacies of such a large family, but he and his siblings were undeniably tight. The thought of having the triplets in Texas felt right at a soul level.

Dillon paced halfway across the open space and then back again. "It has potential, but don't you think we've got enough on our plates?"

"If we don't seize the opportunity," Callum said, "someone else will. Ashley wants to target a late-spring opening. They can get things up and running plus work out any kinks before the summer tourist season swings into high gear."

Steven pulled his phone from his back pocket. "A guy over in Brenham emailed me about a barn that's being torn down. He's got almost a dozen pallets of reclaimed wood." He passed the device to Dillon, who then handed it to Callum.

"That would be perfect for the bar and an accent wall," Callum said, glancing from the photos on the phone to his brother. "I bet the girls would love it."

"I was thinking the same thing," Steven agreed.

Dillon had taken a few steps away, his back to them. Frustration pricked along Callum's spine. He didn't want to move forward without having both his brothers on board. The company was busier than ever since he'd moved operations to Rambling Rose. The pace of business would take all three of them working together in order for it to be a success. Failure wasn't an option.

If Dillon shot down the idea for their sisters to open a restaurant, Callum would respect that. He might be the company's founder, but it was a partnership now.

His younger brother spun around, meeting Callum's worried gaze with an unreadable expression. They stood like that for several seconds until Dillon gave a barely perceptible nod. "If we keep the pipes and ventilation ducts exposed, that will cut costs and make installation simpler. The concrete floor needs to be cleaned and polished, so insulation, electrical and plumbing are going to be the biggest hurdles, assuming there's no structural damage."

Callum and Steven exchanged a fist bump.

"What's that about?" Dillon demanded, eyes narrowed.

"I'm all about the big picture," Callum explained. "Steven goes right to design. You're the detail guy. If you're already working out the HVAC systems, that means you think the project is a go."

Dillon rolled his eyes. "Of course it's a go. What the triplets want, they get. Besides, once the 'big picture' guy is set on something, the rest of us make it happen. How do you think we ended up in this tiny speck of a town in the first place?"

"Not so tiny once we're through," Callum pointed out. "The Fortune brothers are putting Rambling Rose on the map."

"Does that mean you're going to stay?" Steven asked,

his tone casual. "After all the current projects are up and running?"

Callum shrugged, irritation making him twitch. Of course he wasn't going to stay in Rambling Rose. He'd made certain that long-term ties weren't part of the equation since the end of his marriage. He wouldn't take the chance of hurting someone the way he had his ex-wife or opening himself to that kind of pain. But ever since his night with Becky, it felt like his priorities had been turned upside down.

He'd spent so long making his career the most important thing in his life because that kept him safe and in control. His growing feeling for Becky and her girls scared the hell out of him, and moving on would be the quickest way to keep them in check.

"I'm scheduled to drive over to a little town on the eastern edge of San Antonio next week," he said by way of an answer. "It's long past its heyday, but has great bones and easy access to the interstate. The place has potential."

One of Steven's thick brows lifted. "We were under the impression your relationship with Becky had potential, as well."

Dillon cleared his throat. "Couldn't help but notice your headlights coming down the driveway in the wee hours most nights. And a few early mornings."

"Are you a vampire now?" Callum asked.

"Light sleeper," Dillon said with a chuckle.

"You need to move into one of the guesthouses," Callum suggested, not bothering to hide his annoyance.

"Who would have coffee ready for you in the morning?" Dillon shot back.

"Manny," both Steven and Callum said at once, referring to the older caretaker who had come with the property. Manuel Salazar had worked at the ranch for decades. He had a gift with horses and happened to be a decent cook, as well. Callum and his siblings had come to rely on Manny to manage the property and their lives.

Dillon sniffed. "His coffee tastes like tar."

"But he serves it with the best huevos rancheros I've ever had," Steven countered.

"I won't argue that," Dillon admitted. "And no one better tell him I dissed his coffee. I've almost got him convinced to share his green chile recipe with me."

"Becky loves green chile," Callum murmured, remembering how excited she'd been when he'd brought a taco casserole to her house two nights earlier. He'd felt like a bit of a slouch admitting that an employee had actually done the cooking, but she hadn't seemed to care.

"Come on."

Callum stumbled a step as Steven brought him back to the present moment with a shove. "What?" he demanded.

"You like this woman," Steven said.

"Maybe even more than like," Dillon added, doing an annoying shimmy across the dirty floor.

"Shut up," Callum told both his brothers. "We're hanging out. She's nice. It's nothing more."

"Oh, look at that." Dillon pointed at him. "Your pants are on fire."

"Because you're a liar," Steven said helpfully.

"I get the reference." Callum felt a muscle start to tick in his jaw. "You both need to mind your own business."

"Our business is you," Steven said. "That's the way it works with family. Don't act surprised. Especially after you decided to buy a building for the express purpose of helping the triplets."

Callum blew out a breath, his annoyance disappearing. It would be great to have his younger sisters living in Rambling Rose.

"No more talk about my love life," he told them. "Let's discuss restaurant plans. I'm less likely to punch you that way."

Both his brothers laughed. "We'll let you off the hook," Dillon said.

Steven nudged him again. "For now."

Callum would take whatever kind of reprieve he could get.

Chapter Nine

"I'm not sure about this," Becky whispered, more to herself than anyone else.

"My sister's the best hairstylist in Rambling Rose," Sarah Martensen told Becky the following evening. "Brandi is an expert at color."

That vote of confidence did little to ease Becky's nerves, but she smiled. At this point, she sat in a stranger's basement hair studio, with the twins being entertained by Brandi's teenage daughter in the adjacent space. She'd wanted to update her look and remembered Sarah offering to babysit during the pediatric center's opening.

Becky had gotten to know Sarah's husband, Grant, well over the past couple of weeks. The building manager for the pediatric center, he was the kind, paternal type of man she would have wished her girls to have for a grandfather.

With few other options, she'd asked him for his wife's number and called Sarah to see if she would be willing to babysit while Becky got her hair cut and colored. She hadn't sported a real style since the girls had been born.

Sarah had immediately suggested that Becky make an appointment with Brandi, her younger sister, who'd recently opened a hair salon out of her home. It was a simple room in her basement but had all the essentials as far as equipment and supplies.

A benefit was that she'd been able to bring her daughters with her. Sarah had planned to watch them, but Brandi's sweet teenager, a senior at Rambling Rose High School, had captivated the twins.

"I'm going to make you so beautiful," Brandi promised with a wink, "that the handsome Fortune is going to fall at your feet."

"Brandi, hush," Sarah told her sister on a rush of breath.

Becky felt her eyes go wide. "How did you know I was doing this for Callum?"

Sarah shrugged, looking ten kinds of self-conscious. "Grant mentioned that the boy has been stopping by to visit you on the regular."

"He has business at the pediatric center," Becky protested weakly. It wasn't as if she and Callum were trying to keep their relationship—or whatever they'd call it—a secret. But it still felt odd to know people were discussing her personal business. The perils of small-town life, she supposed.

"My husband says Callum Fortune is quite taken with you." Sarah giggled like a schoolgirl. "To be honest, I don't know how you get any work done. I'd spend my days waiting for him."

"I love my job," Becky told them. She didn't bother to mention that she also loved Callum. Hair salon small talk was one thing. Revealing her biggest secret was quite another. "It's nice that he visits, but we're just having fun."

"A woman could have a lot of fun with a man like that." Brandi gave a throaty chuckle as she gestured for Becky to stand so she could move the salon chair in front of the sink attached to the wall. As Brandi turned on the water, Becky sat again, leaning back to rest her neck on the basin.

It felt strangely indulgent to have another person rinsing her hair. Brandi tugged at the thin strips of foil, then used a shampoo that smelled like lavender on Becky's hair. She closed her eyes and let out a blissful sigh.

Would Callum notice the change? In a way it didn't matter. She appreciated this small bit of pampering. It had been too long, she realized, since she'd taken care of herself. She hadn't even taken a vitamin since her jar of prenatal gummies had run out just after the girls were born. Luna and Sasha would continue to be her priority, but it was past time she started taking care of herself as well as them.

Not just with Callum as a motivator, but because she wanted her girls to see that joy and fun were an important part of life.

All too soon, Brandi turned off the water and tapped Becky's shoulder to indicate she could sit up.

"That was the most luxurious thing I've done in ages," Becky told the sisters, prompting them to share an incredulous look.

"Maybe Callum Fortune isn't as much fun as he

looks," Sarah said, both women dissolving into fits of laughter.

Color rushed to Becky's cheeks. "Not counting Callum," she muttered.

"Atta girl," Brandi said as she toweled off Becky's hair.

The next half hour rushed by in a blur of snipping scissors and small talk. Every few minutes, Sarah peeked out of the salon to confirm Brandi's daughter was still entertaining the girls. In this makeshift cocoon of feminine camaraderie, Becky suddenly felt connected to the Rambling Rose community in a way she hadn't since making her home in the small town.

Her status as a widow and single mother had defined her, and she'd allowed it to keep her from truly becoming close to people. A part of her expected everyone to judge her in the same way her parents had. Her mom and dad had never believed she could make a life for herself on her own. She'd wanted to prove them wrong, but in her quest for self-reliance, she'd cut herself off from making real friends in the process.

Brandi and Sarah were decades older than Becky, but the women made her feel like part of their tribe.

Becky was so lost in thought it took her a few seconds to really focus on her reflection in the mirror when Brandi finally spun her around to see her finished hair.

"It's gorgeous," she whispered, reaching up a careful hand to touch the soft strands. Instead of the one-dimensional brown she'd known her whole life, now her hair was subtly highlighted with strands of gold and auburn. The cut was layered around her face, but still hung over her shoulders in a way that looked both effortless and stylish. "You really are a genius with hair."

Brandi gave her a quick hug from behind. "Sweetie, my job is easy when I have someone as pretty as you in the chair." She undid the black smock covering Becky and gave her a hand mirror to inspect the back.

Becky swallowed down the emotion that welled up in her throat. She felt beautiful for the first time in ages, like she was still a woman and not just a mommy.

She paid Brandi, then walked out of the tidy hair salon room. The twins were curled into Brandi's daughter's lap, while the girl read them one of the board books Becky had brought over in the diaper bag.

"Mama," Luna called, scrambling up to toddle over to Becky.

She crouched down to hug her daughter, then glanced at Sasha, who studied her with a wary expression. "It's still Mommy, sweetheart," she said gently.

Sasha's features relaxed and she held up her arms. "Mama."

"Your girls are adorable," Sarah said as they walked up the stairs. "But I didn't get much of a chance to watch them."

"They're so sweet," Lilly, Brandi's daughter, murmured. "I hope I have twins someday."

"Shush your mouth," Brandi told her daughter in an exasperated tone. "I don't want you thinking about babies for another decade."

The girl groaned. "Duh, Mom. I'm just saying—"

"Don't say another word." At the top of the stairs, Brandi wrapped Lilly in a tight hug. "You're going to give me a heart attack otherwise."

Becky laughed at the obvious affection between mother and daughter. She hoped she'd have that kind of open relationship with her girls one day.

She said goodbye with a promise to call Sarah if she needed a babysitter and headed home. Callum had invited her and the twins to dinner at his family's ranch tonight. She felt both nervous and excited about being around the Fortune siblings en masse. While Callum made it easy to forget about the differences in their backgrounds, she wasn't certain things would be the same with the rest of the family. But she wanted to know the people who were important to him and see for herself how they interacted. The role he'd played as a caregiver in his family clearly had shaped the man he was today.

He seemed to believe he was a failure at commitment, yet somehow also remained a steadfast rock for his siblings. Who was the real Callum Fortune? The man who was attentive with her girls and so tender and sweet that Becky couldn't help but fall for him? Or the shrewd businessman who'd move onto the next challenge and town instead of putting down roots?

Becky had to figure out the puzzle of Callum before her heart was truly at risk.

"Stop pacing," Stephanie said, dipping a tortilla chip into the guacamole Manny had prepared before heading to his bunkhouse for the night. "You're like a nervous schoolboy."

Callum ran a hand through his hair as he stared out the window above the kitchen sink that offered a view of the long driveway leading away from the ranch. "I *am* nervous," he admitted. "It's weird. I've never really considered our family name or what it means to have money. I don't want Becky to think I'm some kind of rich snob living out here in this gated community."

Stephanie sniffed. "That's right. Women are so turned off by men with money."

He gave her a narrow-eyed glare over his shoulder. "You know what I mean."

"I do," she agreed after a moment. "I always hated girls fawning over my brothers because of our last name. And that was before we landed in Texas where the Fortunes are something of a dynasty."

"She doesn't care about any of that, which is refreshing."

"You really like her." Stephanie stepped closer.

"Is that such a surprise?" he demanded quietly. If his sister wanted to lecture him on getting involved with a single mother or a woman who'd experienced more than her share of tragedy, Callum would put up one hell of a fight.

"No," Stephanie answered without hesitation. "Becky seems great and her daughters are precious. I just can't figure out if this means you're planning to stay in Rambling Rose long term." She put a hand on his arm. "You convinced us to come to Texas, and now it looks like the triplets will be here, too. This town feels like home, Callum. But you've never been one to put down roots."

"Why does everyone keep harping on the future?" He blew out a long breath as dust whirled up at the edge of the horizon and Becky's minivan crested the hill and made its way toward the house. "She and I are enjoying the moments we have together. It doesn't matter to either of us what comes next."

When Stephanie didn't respond, he turned to find her staring at him, arms crossed over her chest and one foot tapping on the floor in apparent exasperation. "You know nothing, Callum Fortune."

He rolled his eyes. "Just be nice tonight. Make her feel welcome."

"You say that as if I'm normally a social ogre. Remember, brother, I'm a proud rescue animal mom. Between the dogs, the cats and the bunny, those twins are going to love me."

With a chuckle of assent, Callum moved past his sister toward the front door. The property was perfect for him and his siblings. It allowed them to be close but still have their own space. He wouldn't have traded it for another home in the area and hoped Becky wasn't overwhelmed by its size.

He jogged down the steps and came around the front of her vehicle just as she climbed out. The afternoon was clear, with only a few puffy clouds floating along the wide expanse of Texas sky. The temperature hovered in the low fifties, cool enough for long sleeves, but still comfortable. He couldn't wait to take the twins to the barn and see their reaction to the horses.

"Wow." He stopped in his tracks as Becky turned to face him.

She tugged self-consciously on the ends of her hair, which had been transformed since the last time he'd seen her. Her chestnut hair now gleamed with gold highlights that gave it a cohesively warm look.

"I got my hair done," she said as if he needed clarification.

"You look beautiful."

"You tell me that every time we're together," she said with a laugh.

"It's always true." He closed the distance between

them and kissed her, threading his fingers through her soft locks. "I like the new do."

"Thanks." She grinned up at him. "It was time for a change."

The style might be a subtle update but the shift in Becky's confidence felt massive. Of course, he liked her no matter what, but was thrilled to see the light in her eyes that made him know she liked her new look.

"Do you two like Mommy's hair?" He took a step toward the open door of the minivan and Luna and Sasha. His chest pinched as both girls kicked and squirmed at the sight of him.

"Cawl," Sasha shouted in her high-pitched voice.

"Up," Luna demanded.

"They're so excited to see you." Becky leaned into the minivan to unstrap the girls. She wore a simple yellow sweater and a pair of snug jeans tucked into cowboy boots.

"The feeling is mutual," he assured her, ignoring the fast thumping of his heart as his sister's words played on repeat in his head. Was he considering staying in Rambling Rose? He couldn't think about the future without sweaty palms and a nagging feeling that he was bound to mess things up with Becky. That's what he did.

He might want to commit, but he knew there was something broken inside him that prevented him from giving himself fully. Too deep of an independent streak perhaps or he lacked the gene for commitment. Either way, he didn't want to consider the idea that he could hurt or disappoint Becky and her daughters. They meant too much to him.

"Are you okay?" Becky asked softly.

He squeezed shut his eyes for a quick moment, then

grinned at her. "Sorry," he said automatically. "It's been a long week with the finishing touches on the Paws and Claws clinic and the triplets' constant barrage of texts and calls with ideas for the restaurant."

"If you want to reschedule dinner…" She bit down on her lower lip, and he cursed himself for the doubt that flashed in her dark eyes.

"Not at all." He lifted his arms, gratified when Sasha reached for him. "I've been looking forward to showing the three of you my home."

Becky took Luna from her car seat, then hit the button on the vehicle's interior to shut the side door. "It's really great." She cleared her throat. "I actually don't think I've ever been in a house this big."

"The footprint makes it seem larger than it is," he assured her, earning a laugh.

"I don't care that you're rich," she told him, going up on her toes to kiss his cheek. "I like you despite the gobs of money, not because of it."

"I wouldn't describe it as *gobs*," he said, looping his free arm around her shoulder.

"Massive piles?" she suggested playfully.

"You're funny."

She giggled. "I try."

"What would you like to see first? The house or the barn?"

"I think the twins would love to visit the animals, if that's possible."

"Anything is possible for you." He dropped another kiss on the top of her head and led the way to the barn that sat adjacent to the main house.

His sister was waiting inside the wide row of stalls that connected to a spacious arena. The previous owner had been a show jumping enthusiast, and although the arena went largely unused by the Fortunes, Callum appreciated having it available. Unbidden, an image of Sasha and Luna a few years from now popped into his brain. They had the same dark hair as their mother and wore matching riding costumes as they trotted ponies around the arena.

He felt a muscle tick in his jaw as he forced away the mental picture. By the time the girls were old enough for riding, he'd be a distant memory to them and their mother.

"I hope you don't mind me crashing your date," Stephanie said, shooting him a curious glance. "I couldn't pass up the opportunity to get my hands on these little cuties."

"It's nice to see you again," Becky said as Luna waved. Sasha, always the more cautious twin, snuggled against the soft fabric of his chambray shirt, but smiled shyly when his sister tickled her leg.

Luna was happy for Stephanie to hold her, and the look of delight on his sister's face gave him a bit of a start. He knew Stephanie liked babies and young children, but the mix of happiness and yearning in her blue gaze as Becky's daughter relaxed into her arms seemed oddly intense. Stephanie wasn't dating anyone seriously, at least as far as Callum knew, but she certainly looked like a woman ready to become a mother.

"Your hair is so great," Stephanie told Becky. "I need a reference for your stylist."

"She's a local," Becky explained quickly, "who works out of her house. I'm not sure she'd be—"

"Perfect." Stephanie grinned. "I'd love to give her a call."

At the sound of a soft whinny, Luna squealed and

Sasha sat upright, her eyes widening. "Do you hear the horsey?" Callum asked.

"That's Buttercup," Stephanie told the girls and Becky. "He likes visitors." She reached into the front pocket of her jeans and pulled out a handful of baby carrots. "And treats."

They walked forward to where the sleek bay had popped his head over the wall of the stall.

"Sweet boy," Becky murmured. "Isn't he a beauty, girls?"

She stepped forward and held out her hand, palm out. The horse snuffled and rubbed against it. The twins watched in obvious awe as their mother loved on the large animal.

"Do you want to pet him?" Stephanie asked Luna gently. "He loves little girls."

"Uh-huh," Luna murmured, spellbound.

Callum stayed back with Sasha, who seemed less willing to investigate the big horse close up. She watched with fascination as Stephanie helped her sister reach out a hand to touch the animal's soft nose.

Buttercup blew out a contended breath, reveling in the attention. Stephanie placed a carrot in Luna's chubby hand and uncurled the girl's fingers so that the horse could snuffle it up.

"I've never seen her look so happy," Becky said with a wide grin.

"She's horse crazy already." Stephanie dropped a gentle kiss on top of the girl's head, then turned to Callum and Sasha. "What about you, sweet girl? Do you want to give Buttercup a treat?"

Sasha looked less confident than her sister but nodded nonetheless and reached for Stephanie.

"I'll trade you," Callum said with a laugh as he and his sister switched twins.

Becky pulled out her phone and snapped photos of the girls taking turns petting and giving carrots to all the horses housed in the barn. When they'd visited with each of them, Stephanie introduced them to her personal menagerie, which included two cats, Violet and Daisy, plus two dogs, Mack and Tallulah, not to mention a bunny named Orville who charmed both her daughters.

By the time they were finished, the girls were sticky, sweaty and covered with a fine coat of dust. Becky beamed from ear to ear, and Callum's heart felt full to bursting.

The rest of the evening was just as perfect. He'd purchased two high chairs in town, which seemed to make Becky inordinately grateful. She slayed him with her low expectations. If he had his choice, he'd give her anything in his power. Except the one thing that deep inside he feared she wanted the most—his heart.

It was getting more difficult by the moment to ignore his inability to commit to making Rambling Rose his permanent home.

Once again, he focused on the present. They ate the chicken fajitas Manny had prepared, and Becky seemed to be entertained by Steven and Dillon. His brothers flirted with her and the twins, and it was obvious she was both delighted and embarrassed by their attention.

They stayed later than the girls' normal bedtime, and Luna and Sasha had already dozed off by the time they loaded them into the car seats. "I'll see you tomorrow," he told Becky as he kissed her under the sliver of moonlight.

She shivered when a breeze kicked up, and he pulled her closer.

"I'm working tomorrow," she told him.

"It's Sunday. You don't work on Sundays." He wasn't fazed at having her schedule memorized. The moments he spent with Becky, even on her lunch break, were always the best of his day.

She laughed. "I know, but one of the other nurses needed the day off for her son's birthday. The girls like going to the day care center, and it shouldn't be busy."

"How about lunch?" he asked.

"You don't have to—"

"Please." He brushed his mouth over hers. "Let me see you again."

"You see me all the time."

"I can't get enough."

She bit down on her lower lip. "That makes me happy."

"You make me happy."

"Lunch tomorrow," she promised. "I should be able to take a break around noon. Does that work?"

"I look forward to it." He smoothed his hands over her cheeks. How could she be so precious to him after such a short time? There was no explaining the deep connection he felt, but no denying it, either. He'd take her to lunch, to dinner. Hell, he'd drive her to the gas station to fill up her minivan if that's what she needed from him.

He watched her drive away, then turned to walk back up the porch steps. Funny how one evening with Becky and her girls had made his big house finally feel like a home.

Chapter Ten

As she and Callum drove toward the pediatric center the following afternoon, Becky stole glances at her fingers entwined with Callum's larger, tanned hand, her heart hammering in her chest. They'd had lunch at the diner in town and then Callum had taken her to see the feed and grain building he'd just bought with a plan for his younger sisters to convert into a restaurant.

More Fortunes were coming to Rambling Rose, causing nerves to bubble up inside her. She wanted to meet Callum's younger sisters, both because he talked so fondly of the triplets and also due to her curiosity about the bond of adult multiples. Would her girls always be as close as they seemed now? She hoped so, and from what Callum had told her, Ashley, Nicole and Megan might provide great insight.

But each time her ties with the Fortune family deepened, she worried about what that would mean when and if Callum decided to leave Rambling Rose.

Although her love for him seemed so sure and strong, she still had no idea how he felt about her. Certainly she knew he cared for her and her daughters. But that was different from being in love. She thought about broaching the subject even though the doubtful part of her heart worried about what answer she might get.

"Looks like trouble at the center," Callum said, his tone laced with concern.

She looked up from their joined hands to the pediatric center's entrance. Two police cars, lights flashing, were parked in front of the building.

Becky's first thought went to her daughters, although she knew Luna and Sasha were safe in the building's secure day care center.

"Will you drop me off in front?" Adrenaline pumped through her.

As soon as Callum pulled to a stop, she bolted from the truck, flashing her employee badge to the officer who stood just inside the sliding doors when it looked like he might stop her.

Grant Martensen stood near the information desk with another officer. Shannon Goering, the young admissions attendant, stood next to him, wiping at her cheeks.

"What's going on?" Becky's instinct was to rush to check on her girls, but she forced a deep breath. Nothing good would come of her panicking. She placed a hand on the woman's arm, wanting to offer comfort for whatever was so upsetting.

"I didn't know," Shannon said miserably, shaking her head. "She wanted to leave the baby and we learned about the Safe Haven law in training. If I thought the mom might be a danger to herself, I would have tried to keep her here."

Becky looked from Shannon to the thin-lipped police officer to Grant.

"The baby's with Dr. Green," the older man said. "He can give you the details."

Relief and worry battled inside Becky as she headed toward the primary care wing. Relief that the crisis was limited to a single child, but concern about the details of that baby's situation. Parker Green leaned against the high counter of the nurse's station as she entered, holding a phone to his ear. He gave her a swift nod and crooked a finger, beckoning her forward.

"Tell me about the baby," she said when he put down the phone, her eyes darting to the exam room with the closed door.

"He's stable." Parker massaged a hand along the back of his neck. "Vitals are good and no signs of neglect."

"How old?" She was already moving past him. "What's the story?"

"Becky, wait." He placed a gentle hand on her shoulder. "It's the little guy from the ribbon cutting."

She blinked, trying to follow his words. There had been no patients at the opening ceremony except...

"The woman in labor," she said, absently rubbing her arms. "Laurel?"

The young doctor nodded, lines of tension bracketing his mouth. "She left a note tucked into the blanket she'd wrapped the baby in. She said he's better off here for a while and she'll be back as soon as she can."

"Where is she now?" Becky's heart broke for a mother who felt so desperate to relinquish her baby.

Thanks to Callum watching the twins, Becky had been the one to stay with Laurel. The woman had been a heartbreaking mix of strength and fragility. She'd seemed terrified about becoming a mother but determined to take care of her baby.

Becky had empathized with her plight on so many levels. It was exactly how she'd felt the moment her water broke with Luna and Sasha. As much as she'd tried to prepare during her pregnancy, panic had fluttered through her chest like a bird caught without shelter in a rainstorm. She hadn't known how she would handle the reality of motherhood, but she had managed due to a deep sense of devotion to her babies.

She didn't for one instant doubt Laurel's love, but Becky also understood that there were so many factors that went into successful parenting. If Laurel was experiencing some form of postpartum depression and had no support system, it could force her into an act of desperation.

Like giving up her child.

"The authorities are reaching out to the hospital where she delivered the baby," Parker said, as if reading her mind. "The law provides for anonymity, but they want to make sure she's not a danger to herself. Shannon said Laurel seemed to be coherent, but the note mentions the history of the Fortune's Foundling Hospital. It's as if she believes she was leaving the baby at a modern-day orphanage."

A sick feeling spread through Becky's stomach, but she forced herself to focus on what she could do to help. "Can I see the baby?"

"Of course," Parker answered immediately. His phone rang at the same moment. "I've got to take this.

I'm trying to coordinate a plan with the Department of Human Services."

Foster care. Becky drew in a sharp breath at the thought of the tiny infant going to a stranger. Then she reminded herself there were amazing families involved in the foster care system in Texas. If Laurel felt she needed to relinquish her baby, she must have had a good reason, and the welfare of the child was critical at this stage.

She pushed open the exam room door, surprised to find the space empty other than a portable bassinet situated at one end. Her rational side understood. The child's arrival on a low-staffed Sunday afternoon had thrown the pediatric center into crisis mode.

But the mother in her roared in silent disapproval. This baby had been abandoned. He needed someone with him. On instinct, she dimmed the lights, knowing that a baby born only a few weeks ago needed the calmest environment she could provide.

A soft coo from the bassinet had her hurrying forward. She paused long enough to wash her hands in the exam room's small utility sink. One of the other nurses had swaddled him in a hospital blanket and placed a tiny blue cap on his head. He looked like a squirming burrito.

"Hello, big guy," Becky said gently, reaching out to stroke a finger across the boy's cheek.

He immediately turned toward the touch, his rooting reflex kicking in, and she realized he was hungry.

The door to the exam room opened, and Sharla entered, holding a bottle. "Poor little dude." She frowned. "He doesn't have any idea what's going on."

"I'll feed him," Becky offered immediately. "There

has to be some explanation. I talked to the mom during her labor. She seemed overwhelmed, but it was clear she loved her baby even then."

"Who knows," the other woman murmured, handing the bottle to Becky. "My hormones got all out of whack after Thomas was born. It took months of me crying on the bathroom floor before my husband insisted I talk to the doctor. She helped me, but this munchkin's mom was totally alone. Maybe she didn't have anyone to tell her she'd be okay."

"I wish I would have been here when she came in today." Becky lifted the baby into her arms, then took a seat on the bench meant for family members waiting with a young patient. "Maybe I could have helped. Did the note give any details about his care?"

Sharla shook her head. "We don't even know if he was breast- or bottle-fed. All we can do now is try to keep him healthy and hope they track down the mom or find an amazing foster care placement for him."

The baby sucked greedily from the bottle, his tiny fingers grasped on to the front of Becky's scrub shirt. "Does he have a name?" she whispered, tears pricking the back of her eyes at his vulnerability and resilience.

"There wasn't anything in the note about a name." Sharla sighed. "We know Laurel is the mom, so he started out as Baby L. I'm calling him Linus on account of the blue blanket he was wrapped in when he got there."

Becky fingered the soft white fabric that swaddled him now. "Where is that blanket?"

"We got him a fresh one. Figured the blue one might be in need of a good washing."

"Don't do that. It probably smells familiar."

"Do you think she'll come back?" Sharla asked softly. "His mama?"

"I hope so, but more than anything I hope she's okay." Becky maneuvered baby Linus onto her shoulder and gently patted his back until he let out a robust burp. "He's eating like a champ."

The door to the room opened again, and Callum peeked in. "Parker filled me in on the situation," he said gravely.

"You can keep the two of them company," Sharla told him, moving toward the door. "I need to check on another patient."

Callum washed his hands without being asked, then came to sit next to Becky.

"Can you take him for a minute?" she asked. Now that it was just her and Parker, she was having trouble holding back tears.

"Sure." Parker easily transferred the baby to his arms, then took the half-full bottle and offered it to Linus.

"I don't understand how this happened," Becky whispered, wiping at her eyes. "I know Laurel loves him."

Parker's mouth thinned. "She obviously felt like she couldn't care for him the way he needed."

"She should have asked for help."

"That's not easy for some people," Callum reminded her.

Becky knew that all too well. Sometimes it felt like she'd muscled through those first few months of mothering twins on willpower alone. Like Sharla, she'd cried almost every day from sheer exhaustion, but hadn't wanted to admit to anyone how she was struggling for fear they'd judge her or deem her unfit to care for her girls. Looking back, she understood all three of them would have been better off if she'd asked for help.

Even now, she struggled to reach out even though the friends she had in the Rambling Rose community seemed happy to rally around her.

"What's going to happen to him?" Callum asked as the baby finished the bottle. Becky was amazed at how naturally he handled the infant. He'd told her how much responsibility he'd taken on with his younger sisters. Obviously, those skills were deeply ingrained in him. He didn't miss a beat with burping Linus, even thinking to pull a towel off the counter to flip over his shoulder.

Becky glanced down at her own shoulder and cringed at the wet spot of spit-up. She'd never been great at remembering a burp cloth. "Do you mind sitting with him for a few minutes while I get an update from Dr. Green?" She used the edge of her sleeve to dab at the corner of one eye. "I'd also like to take a look at the note Laurel left. I'm hoping something helps me make sense of this whole thing."

She took a step toward the door without waiting for an answer, shock making her feel fragile.

"Becky." At the sound of her name in his deep voice, she stilled.

He came up behind her and pressed a kiss to the top of her head. "It's not your fault."

How did he know what she was thinking?

Drawing in a steadying breath, she turned and glanced down at Linus in Callum's strong arms. The baby had fallen back asleep, lulled by a full stomach and the feeling of security he no doubt had being held by Callum.

"What if I had done more?" she asked, realizing she

sounded as miserable as she felt. "I could have offered to go along with her in the ambulance..."

"You had the twins with you that day," Callum pointed out gently. "I have mad babysitting skills and an insanely trustworthy face, but I doubt you would have just left them with me indefinitely."

"Mad skills," she repeated with a soft laugh. "In so many areas."

When he wrapped his free arm around her, she rested her head against his chest, the steady beat of his heart calming her slightly.

"I could have followed up with her," she said against his shirtfront. "I've thought about her so many times since that day. I saw a lot of myself in Laurel and her situation. What if I'd intervened and given her the support she needed to not give up on herself?"

"You still could," he told her. "There's no telling what will happen next. Hopefully, they find her quickly and get her the help she obviously needs. If that happens, Laurel and Linus will benefit from any support we can give them. Until then, this little guy is most important."

"You're smart, ridiculously handsome and have mad skills as a baby whisperer. Remind me again why you haven't been scooped up by some lucky lady?"

She meant the question as a joke to lighten the mood but knew she'd miscalculated when his body went rigid.

"I'm a bad bet in the commitment department," he said without emotion, taking a step away from her, his gaze shuttered.

She wanted to argue. To tell him that he just needed to believe in himself and to find a woman willing to take a chance on love with him. She could be that woman if he'd let her.

But Callum was right. Linus had to be the priority at the moment, the way Luna and Sasha were always first in Becky's heart and mind. If Laurel couldn't give her baby what he needed, Becky would make sure the community stepped in to help until the situation could be resolved.

"I think you're the perfect bet," she murmured, then quickly left the room, not wanting to gauge his response to her comment.

Dr. Green—or Parker, as he'd told her on multiple occasions to call him—was still at the nurses' station. He ended another call as she approached.

"How is he?"

"He just took down two ounces like a champ." She gave what she hoped was a reassuring smile. "We're going to take care of him."

"That boy will need our care." Parker spoke absently, almost more to himself than her. "It could be a rough road for such an innocent baby."

Becky couldn't allow herself to consider that possibility. She needed to stay focused on resolving the situation. "Any leads on tracking down Laurel?"

Parker's jaw tightened. "She relinquished the baby," he said quietly.

"Temporarily," Becky clarified. "Her note specified that. It's what she told Shannon, as well. She needed a temporary reprieve."

"I understand. But the point of the law is to offer a safe option for the baby that also protects the parent who can't care for him."

"Temporarily," Becky repeated, enunciating each

syllable. "You were here when she came in the first time, Parker. You know as well as I do that she loves her baby. I don't know what Laurel is going through at the moment, but she needs our help and support as much as Linus does."

"Unless the hospital in San Antonio doesn't believe she's a threat to herself, the authorities won't aid in the search for her," he explained, his voice tight. "That isn't how it works when someone voluntarily gives up a child."

"She left him at what she believed was a decades-old orphanage." Becky threw up her hands. "She's confused and she could even be suffering from postpartum depression. We can't just abandon her."

Parker drew in a deep breath, closing his eyes for a moment as if he were deep in concentration. He returned his strained gaze to hers. "We're on the same side, Becky. I want to find and help Laurel and reunite her with Linus if that's what's best for the child."

She opened her mouth to argue that of course being with the mother was best, but she'd worked in pediatrics long enough to know that wasn't always the case. Still, nothing could shake her belief that Laurel would be a good mother if given the chance and the support she needed.

"Where does that leave us?" She pressed a trembling hand to her chest and forced herself to ask the question that had been burning a hole in her gut for the past few minutes. "What happens to Linus now?"

"I've talked to a half-dozen people from social services already." Parker looked past her toward the exam room where she'd left the baby with Callum. "He'll need to be placed with a foster family, and we'll make sure it's someone who will give him the right kind of care." He thumped a hand on the top of the counter, clearly frustrated at not being able to come up with an easy fix for the situation. "Let's go take another look at Baby L."

"We're calling him Linus." Becky fell in step with him. "Callum is with him now."

Parker gave her a funny look. "I wouldn't have expected Callum Fortune to be so comfortable with a baby."

"He took care of his triplet sisters when he was younger." Becky couldn't help the pride that swelled in her tone. "He's really great with kids."

She opened the exam room door to find Callum just finishing up a diaper change for the baby.

"He does diaper duty, too," Parker murmured behind her, chuckling softly. "This one might be a keeper, Beck."

Tension gathered between her shoulder blades at the way Parker's teasing words made her heart leap. She should know better than to allow herself to daydream about the future, but with Callum she couldn't help it. In the weeks and months after her husband's death, Becky had resigned herself to a life with Luna and Sasha as her only focus. She had to be both mom and dad for them, and she'd become accustomed to the loneliness that sometimes found her in the rare quiet moments.

Callum filled that void, but she had to keep reminding herself their relationship was only temporary. He knew how to make her feel special and was a natural with her girls, but when his work in Rambling Rose was finished, he'd move on. If she wasn't careful, he'd take her heart with him when he left.

"All systems are a go for this little trouper," Callum reported, cradling Linus in his arms once again. "What's the plan?"

Parker shook his head. "Social services can't arrange a foster placement until tomorrow morning, so I think he's going to be a guest of the pediatric center tonight."

"I could take him home," Callum said.

Becky felt her mouth drop open, shocked at his willingness to step in. By the way color tinged his cheeks, she had a feeling he was just as surprised at his offer.

"I know I'm probably not the first choice to be responsible for a baby," he clarified, his tone almost self-deprecating in its casualness. "But we might as well take advantage of all that training I had with my younger siblings."

"Callum would take good care of him," she told Parker, hoping Callum knew how much his actions meant to her. Linus was a precious boy but not a child with whom Callum had a personal connection. It was just the kind of man he was to take on a virtual stranger's baby because it was the right thing to do.

"I'm sure you're right," Parker said, giving Callum a tight smile. "Unfortunately, that's flaunting protocol a bit too flagrantly, even for a small-town medical center." He stepped closer to peer down at the sleeping baby. "It's not ideal, but baby Linus will be spending the night with us. I'll make sure the nurses on duty take good care of him."

"Then I'll stay." Callum's hold on the baby tightened ever so slightly. "If it's okay with you? That way we'll know someone is with him at all times."

Parker appeared marginally affronted by that. "You

can stay if you'd like, but rest assured my staff does an exemplary job of caring for our patients."

"I have full confidence in your staff," Callum said, his gaze darting to Becky. "I'll still stay."

"Your choice." The men shared a silent look that Becky couldn't interpret but somehow eased the tension crackling between them. It was as if they'd come to an understanding, and Becky felt her heart go soft at the sight of these two strong men bonding over the care of an abandoned infant.

"I'll have our largest room made up with a bed for you," Parker said before leaving them alone again. "Thanks, Callum. We all appreciate it."

As the door shut behind the doctor, Becky checked her watch, then let out a frustrated sigh. "I have a short shift today because the day care center closes early on Sunday." She offered a wan smile. "I'd rather not bring the girls to see him since he seems to have settled in so peacefully. The last thing this baby needs is more unfamiliar stimulation at this point."

"It's fine." Callum pressed a swift kiss to her mouth. "I'm going to text my brothers and Stephanie and let them know I won't be home tonight. The nurses will take care of both Linus and me tonight."

"I know," she said softly. "It's an amazing thing you're doing."

He chuckled. "I'm sleeping on a hospital bed for the night. Not quite hero material."

"You are to me," she blurted, then felt her cheeks heat as a look of panic passed over his face. "I'll check in later," she said quickly, careful not to meet his gaze. The emotions churning inside her from the baby's plight were making her speak without thinking. She'd been careful not to push Callum more on his future plans. She had to believe that his willingness to become involved with Linus meant he was ready to commit to Rambling Rose. He cared about this town, and she hoped he cared about her, as well.

Chapter Eleven

Callum woke the next morning to the sound of his sister's soft singing and the smell of fresh coffee. Stephanie stood in front of the bassinet, blocking his view of the sleeping infant.

He scrubbed a hand over his eyes and they focused on Becky entering the room. She walked over to him and gently swept her fingers along his jaw, then kissed the top of his head. Her touch was comforting in a way that pricked along his nerve endings. Last night had made him far too vulnerable, more than he'd expected or felt equipped to handle.

He'd told her yesterday he wasn't a hero. He'd simply gone with his natural instinct to protect little Linus, whose young life had changed irreparably in an instant. Coupled with his need to ease the tension he saw in Becky, he'd had no choice but to get involved.

It wasn't the man he knew himself to be, and his greatest fear at this point was that she would expect from him something he wasn't capable of giving.

"Why aren't you in the bed?" Becky frowned as he stretched his neck and sat up straighter in the chair where he'd spent most of the night.

"I was afraid of falling asleep too deeply and not hearing him," he admitted. "What time is it?"

"Almost seven." Becky handed him a cup of coffee. "Stephanie and I arrived at the same time. You look like you could use this."

"Intravenously," he said with a laugh.

"Did Linus wake a lot?" Stephanie asked over her shoulder as she leaned down to pick up the baby.

"Every three hours like clockwork," Callum said, marveling at the care with which his sister held the small baby. Once again, he was struck by the maternal side he hadn't realized was part of Stephanie's makeup. "Bottle, diaper change and some deep conversations about life. The little man and I covered all the bases."

He took Becky's hand, brushing a kiss across her knuckles. "Where are the twins? I thought it was your day off so they wouldn't be coming to day care."

"A friend is watching them." At his raised brow, she added, "It's Sarah, the building manager's wife. She's really good with them, and I wanted to check in on you and Linus."

"I took a personal day," Stephanie said, finally turning toward them. "I couldn't stay away."

"Since when has your biological clock been ticking like a gong?" Callum asked his sister.

"She cares about Linus and Laurel." Becky pushed a

brown paper bag toward him with more force than was necessary. "She's got a big heart."

"Yeah," Stephanie agreed, her eyes narrowing. "Listen to your girlfriend, Callum. She's obviously the brains between the two of you."

He tried to hide the agitation that rose to the surface at Stephanie referring to Becky as his girlfriend. Of course she was his girlfriend. What else would he call a woman with whom he spent almost every night?

But something about the word gave their relationship a gravity that made his flight instinct kick into high gear. Or maybe it was just his lack of sleep. Either way, he busied himself with opening the bag and pulling out a foil-wrapped burrito.

"It's from the food truck out near Mariana's," Becky told him, her voice unusually light. "Best breakfast in town."

Callum wasn't familiar with Mariana's but didn't ask, unsure how to handle the strange current of tension running between them. If Stephanie noticed the awkwardness, she didn't mention it, all of her attention focused on the baby.

The door opened and Parker walked in, his gaze tracking between the three of them. "Then you've heard the news," he said to Becky and Callum before turning to Stephanie. "You're doing a wonderful thing."

"Holding a baby?" Callum scoffed in the way of big brothers everywhere. "She's not that impressive. Wait until she deals with her first blowout diaper."

"There'll be plenty of time for that," Parker said. "As soon as the social worker gets here, we'll finalize the paperwork."

Callum finally glanced up at Becky, who looked as confused as him. "What paperwork?" he asked.

"I haven't told them," Stephanie said, biting down on her lower lip.

"What's going on?" Callum rose from the chair, placing the coffee and breakfast on the counter. He didn't like the way Dr. Green was looking at his sister, like they shared some kind of secret.

"It's not really my news to tell," Parker said carefully. "I'll give you all some time. Stephanie, come to my office when you're ready and we'll go over a few items."

"Ready for what?" Callum demanded as the doctor closed the door behind him.

"Hush," Stephanie whispered when the baby stirred in her arms. "You're going to wake him."

"I should go, too." Becky took a step toward the door, but Callum instinctively reached out and enclosed her thin wrist with his fingers. He might bristle about putting a label on what was between them, but that didn't change the fact that he wanted her at his side.

"You're overreacting for nothing," Stephanie said, then transferred her gaze from Callum to Linus. "I've been approved as this sweetheart's foster mom."

Callum felt his mouth drop open. He looked to Becky, who seemed as bewildered as him. "Since last night?" He shook his head. "That's impossible. It takes—"

"Months," Stephanie finished. "I put in my application right when we moved. I've gotten background checks, gone through interviews." She looked up at him and cringed. "I even did a home visit that weekend in November when you, Steven and Dillon went camping."

"I don't understand." Callum prided himself on knowing every intricacy of his siblings' lives, especially Stephanie and the triplets. They'd always been close. How could she have undertaken something so monumental without telling him about it? "Do Mom and Dad know?"

"I called them this morning," his sister answered, her tone thick with emotion. How had their parents reacted to the news?

He ran a hand through his hair, fatigue and frustration threatening to engulf him. "You shouldn't have done this without running it by the family first."

Stephanie's shoulders went rigid. She carefully placed Linus into the bassinet, then took the few steps across the room to stand in front of Callum. At the same time, he felt Becky shift closer and was profoundly grateful for her sweet protectiveness, even if it was unnecessary.

As one of eight kids, Callum was well versed in sibling squabbles. He loved his family beyond measure and knew they could disagree and still maintain their closeness. But he'd never seen a fire like the one that glowed in his sister's eyes at the moment.

"I'm an adult," Stephanie said, her hands on her hips, her voice like a laser cutting through him. "Don't forget, I'm only a few years younger than you. So as much as I appreciate the big-brother-knows-all routine, you don't know everything about me. I make decisions for my life based on what is right for me." She tapped her chest with two fingers. "I'm going to be that baby's foster mom, and I will care for him like he's my own as long as he needs me."

"This will change everything," he said, although he wasn't sure whether he spoke the words for her benefit or his own. "Paws and Claws is about to open. You'll be busy with that. There's so much going on. Fostering Linus is going to—"

"Give my life more meaning," she interrupted, a gentle catch in her voice. "It will make me happy and challenge me in ways I probably can't imagine." Stephanie laughed softly. "I know what I'm getting into, Callum. You might not be ready to settle down and build a life and home in Rambling Rose, but I am."

Becky let out a startled gasp next to him, but he couldn't take his eyes off his sister. It was like seeing her for the first time, or at least seeing her in a different light. Only a few years separated them in age, but he'd taken on a protective role toward her as much as he'd had with the triplets. Now they'd all grown up.

Ashley, Megan and Nicole were going to open their restaurant in Rambling Rose, linking three more members of his family to this community. And Stephanie was becoming a foster parent to a sweet, innocent baby who needed her. Linus would be living under their roof until his future was settled. Was that odd pain in his gut the uneasy feeling of his siblings passing him by?

He'd thought he knew what he wanted from life, but now questions and doubts swirled through him like a cold gust of wind. He didn't know how to buffer his heart from the potential damage other than to close it off.

All he could control was his reaction to the present moment, and right now he understood he needed to change his attitude. He might not understand Stephanie's reasons for choosing this path, but his only job was to support her on it.

"I'm sorry," he said gently. "Blame it on sleep deprivation or—"

"Your typical high-handedness," she added, but one side of her mouth curved into a smile.

"That, too," he admitted. "You will be the most amazing foster parent. All of us, and especially Linus, are lucky you made that decision." He ran a hand through his hair. "It's one of the most selfless things I can imagine, and I'm actually in awe of you right now."

Stephanie sniffled and dabbed at the corner of her eye. "It's about time."

"It really is a gift you're giving baby Linus," Becky added. "If there's anything I can do to help you with the transition, please let me know."

For the first time since she'd revealed her plans, Stephanie looked the tiniest bit panicked. "I'll take you up on that," she told Becky. "I have the best of intentions, but very little experience with infants. And virtually no supplies."

Becky wrapped his sister in a quick hug. "That I can take care of for you."

He could see Stephanie relax and understood that response. Becky's generous spirit and quiet confidence had that effect on him, as well, easing any of the sharp edges of his life and allowing him to enjoy the small moments that meant the most.

"I'd appreciate it so much." Stephanie offered Becky a wide smile. "I'm trying to appear like I know what I'm doing, but inside I'm terrified."

If Callum hadn't felt like a jerk before, that admission sealed the deal. His sister needed his support, not judgment or doubt.

"You'll do great," Becky assured Stephanie. "While you meet with Parker and the social worker, I'll head home and gather up supplies. I didn't find out the sex of the twins during the pregnancy, so I still have tons of neutral baby clothes. I'll meet you at the ranch and get Linus settled in with you."

Stephanie nodded. "Thank you. I just realized I don't even have a car seat for him." She shook her head. "What kind of foster parent doesn't have a car seat?"

"The kind who wanted to meet her tiny charge right away." Becky squeezed Stephanie's arms, then took a step toward the door. "We keep a couple of infant seats stored in the utility closet next to the day care center in case patients need them."

"I'll go get it," Callum offered, needing to feel useful in some way. "Then I'll call Steven and Dillon to explain what's going on." He flashed a wry smile at his sister. "I can at least save you from having to deal with them the way you did me."

"It's probably good that your initial reaction was so lame." Stephanie winked. "Now you'll feel guilty about it for weeks and will happily do diaper duty or late-night feedings to make it up to me. Right?"

He wrapped her in a tight hug. "Whatever it takes, li'l sister."

Becky tried to focus on the twins' happy babbling from the back seat as she drove toward the ranch and not on the disappointed beating of her own heart.

All those silly fantasies she'd had of Callum had evaporated like dew on the grass in the morning sun. Listening to him speak to his sister about losing her freedom made Becky know that he wasn't thinking of staying. At least not now.

She had no idea how he felt about her and her girls. Sure, he liked spending time with them. And the way he touched her body in the quiet hours of night made her feel cherished. But was it all just a temporary arrangement for him?

The Fortunes were doing so much for Rambling Rose. She hated to think that he could easily move on after all the work they'd put into revitalizing the town. She'd heard rumblings that some of the locals weren't happy with all the changes. People were afraid that their community was falling prey to a sort of cowboy gentrification, and that longtime residents would be pushed aside for businesses that catered to the wealthy people moving into areas like the Rambling Rose Estates.

She knew that wasn't the intent of Callum or his brothers. They wanted to add to the community, but if his plan didn't include staying long-term, how much would Callum care about his impact?

And what about the impact he'd already had on her heart, she thought as she pulled up to the gatehouse at the entrance of the gated subdivision.

She offered a smile to the uniformed attendant, who frowned in response, giving her dusty minivan a dismissive once-over.

Acid seeped into Becky's veins. Callum and his family had never made her feel like less because of their differences in social and financial status. The man staring at her now, with his cropped cut and ice-blue gaze, managed to do just that without saying a word. The older gentleman who'd been working the first night she'd come to the ranch was nowhere in sight.

"I'm visiting the Fortunes," she said, forcing a cheerful tone.

"You aren't on the list," he said flatly.

"It's been a whirlwind kind of morning." Becky

hitched a thumb toward the cargo area of her vehicle. "I'm bringing supplies for Stephanie and her new baby. Maybe you heard about the baby relinquished at the pediatric center yesterday? The Fortunes have stepped in to care for him, and I'm helping with that."

She drew in a breath and tried to calm her beating heart. Nerves made her babble, and the way this man looked at her as if she were dirt on the bottom of his boot gave her a feeling of indignity she didn't appreciate.

Sasha began to whimper from the back seat, as if she could sense her mama's tension and wanted to offer her own kind of toddler empathy. Unfortunately, the last thing Becky needed was a meltdown on top of everything else.

"I'm Callum Fortune's girlfriend," she said, changing tactic. "He's expecting me."

"Not on the list," the man repeated. He pointed to a few open parking spaces. "You can turn around over there."

Becky almost did what he told her. That was how she was raised. Listen to authority. Don't make waves. Know your place.

This surly man was a literal gatekeeper. She was tempted to drive home and ask Callum to come and pick up the baby supplies from her house. It would be much easier that way.

If motherhood had taught her one lesson, though, it was that she possessed enough strength that she didn't have to take the easy way out. She understood how to win a battle of wills. If this dude thought he had anything on a pair of grumpy toddlers, he was sorely mistaken.

"I'm not leaving," she said, moving her sunglasses to the top of her head so she could return the gatekeeper's glare. "You can choose to trust me or you can call Callum." When the guy opened his mouth to argue, she held up a hand. "But just so we're clear, he's going to be very angry that you doubted me."

The guard's already pinched mouth thinned even further. After several long moments of staring at the clipboard in his hands, he thrust it at her. "Write down your name, address and phone number. If there are any questions, we'll know how to contact you."

"Okay," she answered and scrawled the information with trembling fingers. It had worked. She'd held her ground and gotten her way. Forcing herself not to cheer or break out in song, she returned the clipboard to him. "You made the right decision today. Thank you."

He gave a brief nod, then went into the gatehouse and hit the button to open the wrought-iron gate.

Becky drove through with a wide grin on her face. "Did you see how Mommy stood up to the rude man?" she asked her daughters, glancing at each of them in the rearview mirror. Sasha stared at her solemnly, binky shoved in her mouth, while Luna stared out the window at the rolling hills. "You girls are going to understand your worth a lot earlier than I did. I'm going to make sure you know that you deserve to be treated well all the time. No exceptions."

She blew out a shaky breath, adrenaline pumping through her at the small stand she'd taken. "We will respect authority, but also know that we should be respected, as well. I'm going to become a strong woman so I can raise strong women." She laughed at the depth of conversation she was having with her daughters.

They couldn't understand the meaning of her message but she continued to speak about their value as she drove down the winding drive that led to the Fortune ranch, needing to say the words out loud for herself as much as for them.

Callum and Steven walked down the porch steps as she pulled to a stop in front of the large house.

"How are Stephanie and Linus?" she asked as she came around the front of the car.

Steven grimaced. "Who knew our sister had the heart of a drill sergeant? She's been barking orders in a weird singsong voice since they got here."

"I don't think she wants the baby to realize that he's being cared for by a foster mom dictator," Callum added with a snort.

The brothers shared a pained look that made Becky stifle a giggle. The combined handsomeness of the two of them almost took her breath away. She knew they were stepbrothers, but the similar way they held themselves showed their family connection. She glanced up as the front door opened and the third of the Rambling Rose Fortune men appeared.

She knew from Callum that Dillon was his full-blood brother. He had sandy-blond hair and was more thickly muscled than the other two, but his features resembled Callum's. She'd met their father only on that one occasion, but both boys looked like David Fortune. She could only imagine the string of broken hearts they'd left in their collective wake and hoped to never be among that group.

"Linus is a lucky boy," Becky said, wanting to show solidarity with Stephanie.

Callum laughed softly. "Good answer."

"She sent us out here to unload the haul," Dillon told her.

Becky hit the button on the key fob to unlatch the back cargo door and then opened the side door to reveal the twins. Both girls looked with wide-eyed curiosity at the trio of handsome men staring at them.

The Fortune brothers could even dazzle ladies still in diapers. Impressive.

Luna clapped her hands as her gaze fell on Callum. "Cawl," she shouted happily.

Sasha pulled her binky from her mouth and squealed his name, as well.

"Nice fan club," Steven told Callum and then followed Dillon to the back of the vehicle.

Becky leaned in to unfasten the girls' car seats, but Callum quickly grabbed her from behind, pulling her close and reaching around to plant a gentle kiss on her throat. "Hi," he whispered against her hair.

"Your brothers will see," she protested, wiggling out of his grasp.

"I'm pretty sure they know I kiss you." He chuckled at his own joke, but released her. "Did you have any problems at the gate?"

She stilled. "Why do you ask?" She threw the questioning glance over her shoulder.

"The new guy is a real piece of work," Dillon said, reappearing with a bouncer seat. "He actually made me show him my driver's license the other night. As if I don't live here."

"I didn't have any trouble," Becky lied. It was easier to let them believe she'd made it through without incident.

"He probably took one look at you," Steven told her

as he hefted a big box of clothes, "and thought he better not mess with a boss mom."

Color rose to her cheeks. "That's me," she confirmed with a grin.

As she spoke to his brothers, Callum had reached around her to get the twins. He lifted Luna out of her car seat and handed her to Becky, then undid Sasha's car seat strap and straightened with the girl in his arms.

"Do you think Stephanie's up for visitors?" she asked, pausing at the base of the porch steps. "If you think she'd rather get settled in peace, I can come back another time."

"I know she'd love to see you," Callum told her with a smile. "She's already started a list of baby care questions for you. I think she's hoping you'll be her expert resource."

"Anything I can do to help." Becky followed him up the steps and he paused to let her enter the house before him.

"I really appreciate—"

When his words cut off, Becky glanced up at him.

"I appreciate you," he said, the intensity of his tone sending shivers down her spine.

She drew in a breath. Maybe she hadn't misinterpreted how he felt. Maybe her heart was safe with Callum after all. Could she dare to believe that?

Chapter Twelve

Callum sat in his truck, finger hovering above the send button on his phone. It was nearly midnight, and he should be home and in bed. The problem was he didn't want to be in his bed, not without the woman whose house he'd been parked outside for the past fifteen minutes.

He'd driven to Becky's on a whim, without a plan for what to do once he arrived. If he texted her, would it look like a booty call? He didn't mean it that way and certainly wanted to avoid giving her that message. Not that holding Becky in his arms wasn't as damn near close to perfection as he could imagine.

But after the unexpected events of the last twenty-four hours, he craved something more. The comfort he found in her arms.

Linus's arrival and the thought of the baby's mother

out there in the world, so desperate that giving up her son felt like the best option, had rocked him to his core. Despite the unrest in his early years from his parents' contentious divorce, Callum had always known love growing up. Marci had come into their lives and immediately taken him and Dillon into her heart.

Even when her health suffered during those years of trying to conceive again and after the triplets' birth, she'd never wavered in her maternal devotion. He'd had two parents who loved him and a gaggle of siblings who made him crazy but also helped him to never feel truly alone.

The baby his sister had taken on had been abandoned in the world. At least for now. He knew Stephanie would do everything in her power to love and protect little Linus. His sister had shown a depth of spirit and service that humbled Callum. He couldn't force himself to commit to staying in Rambling Rose long-term because of the risk of being hurt, or causing pain to someone who loved him, the way he had with Doralee.

He'd never thought of himself as a coward. He'd established his company and grown the business to the point where he could cherry-pick the most appealing projects. His brothers had found a place with him, and he'd naively assumed that his success as a real estate developer and contractor was enough for a fulfilling life.

A couple of hours ago he'd understood how far he truly had to go, and it had terrified him.

A part of him had wanted to cut and run. He'd gotten in his car after an hour of restless tossing and turning, not sure whether to head out of town or just drive until exhaustion sent him home again. Almost unaware of where he was going, he'd ended up at Becky's.

He startled as his phone vibrated now, the tone alerting him to an incoming message.

Are you going to sit in your truck all night or come in?

A text from Becky.

He glanced through his windshield toward the house to see Becky standing at the family room window, the lamp behind her bathing her in light.

His fingers trembled as he typed in a two-letter response.

In.

He climbed out of the truck and headed for the front door, heart pounding.

Becky met him at the door, her honey-colored eyes unreadable. She wore a thin cotton nightgown with two kittens curled together on the front and the words *snooze squad* scrawled beneath them. He must have it bad when he found kittens sexy as hell.

"I know it's late," he said, offering an apologetic smile. "If I woke you I'm—"

His words were cut off when she launched herself at him, wrapping her arms around his neck as she fused her mouth to his.

He lifted her off the ground as he stepped into the house, kicking the door shut behind him. She seemed as frenzied with need as he felt, like she couldn't get enough of him. Her tongue delved into his mouth, and he groaned out loud, almost stumbling at the power of the desire pulsing through him.

Instead of moving toward the bedroom, he detoured into the nearby family room and lowered her to the couch. "I need you so badly," he whispered, shocked by the intensity of his own voice.

"Yes," she answered, smoothing her soft hands across his face. "Please, Callum."

It was as if he'd devolved into some kind of inexperienced schoolboy overwhelmed at the possibility of a night with his biggest crush.

In such a short time, Becky had come to mean so much to him. He still couldn't allow himself to acknowledge the depth of his feelings in his heart or mind, but his body seemed to have no such constraints.

It took only a few seconds to pull the sweatshirt he wore over his head and unfasten the button on his jeans. He paused then because Becky had sat up on the sofa and taken off her nightgown. She sat before him in only a pair of lacy blue panties, the perfection of her body making his mouth go dry.

"You never cease to blow me away with your beauty."

"You should close the curtains," she told him with a slight smile. "Before you give my neighbors a glimpse of a full Fortune moon."

He yanked the ends of the linen drapes together, then kicked off his shoes and pushed his jeans and boxers down over his hips. He grabbed his wallet from his pocket before stepping out of them, taking out the condom packet as he turned back to her.

"It goes both ways," she said as he moved toward her. "The way you look takes my breath away." She bit down on her full lower lip. "And the way you look at me makes me want you more than I thought was possible."

He closed the distance between them and lowered himself over her, taking her mouth in a kiss that he hoped communicated everything he wasn't able to say out loud. As the kisses deepened, he moved his hand down her body, loving the feel of her soft skin and the way she arched into his touch. He cupped one full breast in his palm, skimming his thumb over the sensitive peak.

She moaned, and he caught the sweet sound in his mouth. Then he moved lower, snagging the waistband of her panties with his fingers. Trailing kisses down her throat and chest, he continued to move lower, pushing the scrap of cotton over her hips and lower until she was completely naked under him.

He gently spread her legs and pressed a kiss to the most intimate part of her. She gasped and reflexively stiffened, but he murmured words of encouragement and praise, feeling like he'd won some kind of lottery when she relaxed again.

"Let me have all of you," he told her, glancing up to meet her desire-hazed gaze.

She gave a shaky nod, and he turned all of his attention to pleasing her. With his tongue and lips and fingers he explored her, gratified at the sensual noises she made.

Soon her whispered words became a chorus of *yes* and *please* and his name. When the release broke over her, it was almost his undoing. Her body seemed to come apart with pleasure.

He plucked up the condom packet he'd dropped to the floor, ripped it open with his teeth and then sheathed himself. As he positioned himself above her, she gave him a smile that just about melted his heart. This was how he wanted to make her feel all the time—languid and blissfully content.

She reached for him, opening again and taking the length of him as if they'd been made to fit together. They moved as one and he lost track of where she started and he began. As pressure built inside him, he tried to tamp it down. His needs didn't matter until she was fully satisfied.

Her nails skimmed lightly across his back, sending quivers of need swirling through him. He lost track of time and place, lost in the moment and the joy of sharing it with Becky.

When she finally cried out his name and her body clenched around him, his breath caught in his throat. The release roared through him like a runaway train, pounding euphoria through every cell in his body.

He'd never experienced something so intense, and the force of it caught him off guard. His body tightened for several long seconds as he was suspended in a maelstrom of emotion. As the shockwaves subsided, he lowered his head, nuzzling the side of her neck.

She smelled of citrus and woman, a combination that he would forever associate with Becky.

He almost laughed at the thought that he'd never be able to smell the scent of lemons without thinking of this moment.

She pushed her fingers into his hair, and he lifted his head to drop a kiss on her forehead. "Sorry I ruined your good night's sleep."

She flashed a slow smile. "I'll forgive you this time."

Her eyes darkened. "What brought you here tonight, Callum?"

"I wanted you." He didn't dare try to express to her all the emotions tumbling through him. The level of need he felt. At this point, it was easier if she believed their physical connection had led him to her. Anything more would reveal too much.

She continued to smile but for an instant he would have sworn a shadow passed over her gaze. "I'm glad," she answered, although he got the feeling she wanted to say more.

He didn't want the moment to end but forced himself to get up, grabbing his boxers from the floor. "I'll be right back," he told her, hoping he was imagining the awkwardness suddenly radiating between them.

It took him only a few minutes in the bathroom, and he figured she might have moved to her bedroom in the meantime. Instead, he saw the glow of a light coming from the kitchen.

As he entered the room, Becky gave him a tight smile. "Thanks again for stopping by." She held out his jeans and T-shirt, which she'd folded into a neat pile along with his socks and shoes. "You'll probably want to get dressed before heading out."

"Um…" He frowned but took the clothes from her. "Yeah. Is everything okay?"

"Fine." Another stiff smile. "I have an early day to-morrow, though, so I should get to sleep."

"Sure." He realized he sounded like an idiot with all of his one-word responses, but her actions left him rattled. They'd just shared mind-blowing intimacy, the best of his life. Now she was basically kicking him out.

What the hell?

Instead of arguing or asking for an explanation, he quickly donned his clothes and shoved his feet into the boots. As far as she knew, he'd gotten what he came for and if he wasn't willing to reveal the depth of his feelings for her, he didn't deserve any more.

She stood leaning against the cabinets on the far side of the room, her expression guarded. The adorable kittens on the front of her nightgown seemed to taunt him. They had a place here, and he had a big pile of nothing.

Because he had nothing to offer. And apparently Becky knew it.

"Thanks again for..." What exactly should he say?

Her chest rose and fell on a quick inhalation of breath.

"Everything," he finished softly.

The smile that curved her lips looked forced, but he didn't ask about it. Not when his own emotions felt too jumbled and unsure.

"I'll talk to you tomorrow," she told him as she walked him to the front door. "Or I guess I should say later today."

He sighed. "I'm sorry I woke you tonight." He had to offer something.

"You didn't. I got up to check on the girls and saw your truck out the window. I'm glad I saw you." She shook her head and huffed out a faint laugh. "Otherwise, you could still be sitting at the curb."

Why did he feel like he was being kicked there now?

She gave him a quick kiss after opening the front door. "Good night, Callum."

He said good-night and a moment later stood alone in the darkness of an empty January night.

* * *

"I'm the one who's sleep deprived," Stephanie told Callum later that week as they stood in the front lobby of the veterinary clinic. "Why are you so grumpy?"

"I'm not grumpy," he answered through clenched teeth, earning a laugh from his sister.

When he didn't respond, she sucked in a quick breath. "Tell me there's not another delay for the clinic." She gestured to the men carrying in the new cabinets for installation. "You and Steven managed to avoid one potential disaster. My nerves can't take another one at this point, not with the opening coming up so quickly."

He pulled out his phone and glanced at it for what felt like the hundredth time that morning, then lifted his gaze to Stephanie's. "Everything's on track. The crew will be putting in some long hours, but the facility is going to open on time and be fully functioning." He flicked another look at the annoyingly dark phone screen and then added, "It's all good."

"Something isn't right with you." Stephanie reached out a finger and tapped it on the edge of his phone case. "Are you angry about Linus?"

Callum blinked. "What are you talking about?"

"I get that you had your fill of kids underfoot when we were growing up." She flashed a weak smile. "Even though he's still tiny, it's kind of shocking how much stuff comes along with having a baby. The peacefulness of the house has been disrupted, and I'd understand if you resent the intrusion."

"I don't," he told her, shocked and a bit chagrinned that he'd given off that impression. "Linus is adorable and I meant it when I said you're doing an amazing thing for that baby."

"Yes," she agreed slowly. "But I'm beginning to wonder about Laurel returning. No one has heard from her." Stephanie crossed her arms over her chest. "Of course I'm happy to keep him for as long as needed, but I guess I thought it would be a short-term placement. What if his mama doesn't return to claim him?"

Callum looped an arm around his sister's shoulder. "Then he'll be lucky he's got you as a foster mom. I'm sorry I made you question whether I'm okay with having Linus in the house. Make no mistake, Stephanie. He's where he needs to be, and I support you 100 percent." He squeezed her arm. "The baby routine is an adjustment for all us, but I wouldn't have it any other way." He frowned. "I like babies. Hell, I helped take care of the triplets for years. And Becky's girls love me. Why do people think I'm antibaby?"

She patted a hand against his chest. "That's funny. No one believes that, but you've made it pretty clear that domesticity isn't your cup of tea at this point. I don't necessarily agree with that and would offer Becky and the twins up as evidence to the contrary, but—"

"Do you think that's why she's avoiding me?" he blurted.

Stephanie took a step away from him, inclining her head. "I didn't realize she was, but it certainly explains your mood."

"My mood is fine," he growled.

"Uh-huh. Tell me more about being ghosted."

He ran a hand through his hair, glancing around to make sure no one could overhear them. From Callum's experience, construction workers liked to gossip as much as a posse of teenage girls. The last thing he needed was to be the topic of conversation for his crew.

"I wouldn't call it ghosting. We had lunch once this week and I took her and the girls to dinner last night. She's not ignoring me completely, but there's a distance between us, even when we're together. I can't figure out why or what's causing it."

His sister frowned. "When did it start?"

"After Linus arrived at the pediatric center," he said after thinking on it for a few seconds. "But that doesn't make sense. Becky has a clear attachment to his welfare. I think she bonded with Laurel on that first day."

"Becky has been an amazing support for me," Stephanie said with a nod. "She checks in several times a day and answers every tiny question I have right away. Since he started going to the day care at the center at the beginning of the week, she's made a point of stopping by and sends me updates on how he's doing. I don't get any strange vibes from her."

"Then what could it be?" Callum shook his head, frustrated that he couldn't figure this out. Part of why he was so successful in the renovation business was his love of solving complex problems. With a historic building or old property in need of revitalization, there were always unique challenges that didn't present themselves with new construction. He thrived on managing those kinds of issues. The fact that he couldn't seem to decipher the actions of one woman made him want to shout in frustration.

The toe of Stephanie's boot tapped on the newly installed floor. "Have you been an idiot?"

"What kind of question is that?"

"A valid one based on your defensive tone."

He shook his head. "I don't know. I don't think so. I like her. She likes me. Her girls like me."

"Are you sure *like* is the *L* word you're looking for at the moment?"

"Stop." He held up a hand. "It's been a few weeks. You know what a bad bet I am, Stephanie. We can't rush into anything when I don't even know if I'm staying in Rambling Rose."

She shook her head. "That's your past talking, Callum. Not your future. You know Dad always says it only took him a moment to know Mom was the one. If he'd let his divorce from your mother define him, our family wouldn't be what it is today."

Callum swallowed. How could he explain to the sister who looked up to him that their father was a better man in so many ways?

"Maybe she's just changed her mind about things," he forced himself to say. "I know she was wary of getting involved in the first place because of the twins. They're her priority and I respect that. It could be as simple as Becky not wanting her life complicated."

"You sound pathetic," his sister told him.

He rolled his eyes. "Not at all helpful."

"Could be the kind of help you need is a swift kick in the pants."

"Forget I mentioned anything."

"I want you to be happy," Stephanie said, her tone gentler. "Tell me if there's anything I can do. Maybe I could talk to Becky for you?"

"No." He shook his head. "This isn't junior high where I need you to pass her a note and have her check the box whether or not she likes me."

"I hated those notes," his sister murmured. "So much pressure."

"Yeah." Feeling pressured was exactly his problem at the moment. But he didn't want to push Becky until he felt certain about what he could offer her. If only he could work out the puzzle of his heart, maybe everything else would fall into place.

Chapter Thirteen

Becky sat in front of the computer at the nurses' station entering stats on a recent patient when she felt someone watching her. She looked up to find Sharla and Kristen staring at her from the other side of the counter.

"I didn't eat the last doughnut," she lied without hesitation, wiping a finger across her bottom lip in case any leftover crumbs might give her away.

"We're not here about doughnuts," Sharla said, crossing her arms over her ample chest.

Kristen nodded in agreement. "We just saw Callum Fortune walking out of the building looking like someone stole his new puppy."

"He doesn't have a puppy," Becky muttered, refocusing on the computer.

"What's going on with the two of you?" Sharla demanded. "Don't tell us you're going to waste your chance with a man who is hot, rich and clearly way into you."

Dragging in a slow breath, Becky pushed back from the desk and stood. "I'm not telling you anything. There's nothing to tell."

"We haven't seen the two of you together as much lately," Kristen pointed out, none too helpfully.

"Things are busy around here," Becky countered. "As you'd know if you stopped trying to pump me for information."

Sharla arched a superbly penciled brow. "Defensive much?"

Becky set her jaw and returned the other woman's steely stare. "I'm not…" She paused, concentrating on the air that seemed caught in her lungs like a moth in a spider's web. "I don't know what's going on." She glanced around to make sure no one could overhear their conversation. "I did a really stupid thing."

"You're pregnant again," Sharla guessed, her eyes widening.

"No." Becky shook her head. "I fell in love with him."

Kristen reached out a hand and squeezed Becky's trembling hand. "Oh, honey. You're only human."

Becky laughed. "Right?" she agreed. "The problem is I don't know how he feels about me. I'm not even certain he's planning to stay in Rambling Rose long term. What if I give him my heart and he breaks it?"

Sharla started to answer, then snapped her mouth shut when one of the exam rooms opened and Parker walked out. "We're just waiting on a lab report and then they'll need a follow-up appointment." He approached the desk. "Everything okay here?" he asked, concern in his tone.

"Peachy keen, Dr. Green," Kristen answered.

He must have heard something in her voice that made him wary because he stopped in his tracks and immediately pulled his phone out of the pocket of his white lab coat. "Look at that. I need to return this call. I'm going to just… I need to go my office." He flashed a tight smile. "And close the door."

"We'll hold down the fort out here," Sharla told him.

"I'm going to go check on the family waiting for labs," Kristen said, then pointed a finger at Becky. "Whatever Sharla tells you, that's what you're going to do. No questions asked."

Becky gave a small shake of her head. "I don't know about—"

"No questions," the redheaded nurse repeated.

"Okay," Becky whispered, watching Kristen disappear into the exam room.

Sharla propped her elbows on the desk and leaned in. "Have you told him you love him?"

"Of course not."

"Do you think you might want to start there?"

"What if it freaks him out and he breaks up with me?"

"What if he feels the same way and doesn't know how to tell you because you're acting so strange?"

"I'm not acting…" She clasped a hand over her mouth when a sob tried to break free. "It wasn't supposed to happen like this," she said, more to herself than Sharla. "I already had my love story. Rick was the love of my life. If I tell Callum I love him, am I being disloyal to my late husband? Am I a terrible person?"

"For wanting to be truly happy again after overcoming a tragedy no one should have to face?" Sharla offered a tender smile. "Of course not. You're a good person, Beck, and an amazing mother. I didn't know your late husband, but I can only imagine he'd be proud of the life you'd made for your girls. You deserve happiness."

"Thank you," Becky whispered. She hadn't realized how badly she needed someone to give her that permission until her friend did. "I don't just want to blurt out the words while we're taking turns feeding the twins. I know Callum cares about the girls and they will always be my priority, but I'd like to do something special for him." She shrugged. "Romantic gestures aren't exactly my forte. Any ideas?"

"Oh, girl." Sharla swiped at her eyes, then grinned like the cat that ate the canary. "I've got you covered on romance."

"You need to come with us."

Callum turned from where he was meeting with the foreman at The Shoppes to find Steven and Dillon striding toward him.

"What happened? Is it Linus? Stephanie?" He threw up his hands. "What's going on?"

"Bro, chill. Everything's fine." Dillon gave him a strange look. "You're wound as tight as a top."

"We've got a lot of work going on," he told his brother, gesturing to several dozen pallets of lumber lined against the far wall. "In case you haven't noticed."

"I've noticed," Dillon told him. "And we've got it all covered."

"At least for the next twenty-four hours," Steven added with a smug smile.

"You two aren't making any sense." Callum narrowed his eyes. "Are you drunk?"

"Give us a couple of minutes, Dan," Steven told the older foreman when he chuckled at Callum's accusatory question.

"Sure thing, bosses." The wiry man with a shaggy beard walked toward the space where the electricians were roughing in recessed lighting.

"Seriously, you need to loosen up." Dillon walked behind Callum and half guided, half pushed him toward the door.

"You still haven't explained what's going on," Callum said through clenched teeth. His patience was at an all-time low. He hadn't seen Becky since he'd stopped by the pediatric center yesterday, and she'd done little more than give him a swift kiss before turning her attention back to whatever she was doing on her large desktop monitor.

Not that he expected her to drop her work for him, but he missed her. He missed the closeness they'd had and hated the tension he couldn't quite put his finger on that seemed to pulse between them.

He'd texted her earlier in the morning, but hadn't received a response. And no, he told himself, he definitely wasn't compulsively checking his phone in case he'd missed the tone or vibration of an incoming message.

"Do you trust me?" Dillon asked as he continued to herd him like a farm animal.

"Normally, yes." Callum shrugged off his brother's grasp but continued walking to the building's entrance. "Right now I trust you about as far as I can throw you."

He pointed a finger at Steven, who stood holding open the front door.

"You'll be sorry you doubted us in about ten seconds," his brother warned with a Cheshire cat smile. "What do you think of that Corvette over there?" He gestured toward a vintage sports car parked in the shopping mall's empty lot.

"It's a beauty." Callum squinted at the cherry-red vehicle, shading his eyes from the bright winter sunlight. "Did you buy a…" His voice trailed off as Becky appeared from the driver's side. Her hair tumbled over her shoulders and she offered a tentative wave.

"Waiting for the apology," Steven said with a nudge.

"What's going on?" Callum whispered. "Why is she here?"

"Your girlfriend has more appreciation for romance in her pinkie finger," Dillon said, thrusting a duffel bag into Callum's arms, "than you do in your entire lunkheaded body."

"Becky arranged an overnight getaway for the two of you," Steven explained. "We're covering you for the next twenty-four hours. A smart man would stop asking questions, mute his phone and go kiss the beautiful woman waiting for him."

Callum's mind might be spinning in a thousand different directions, but he wasn't a total idiot. "You two are the greatest brothers in the history of the world. If you tell Wiley I said that, I'll deny it. But thank you."

"Have fun," Steven told him with a grin.

"Don't do anything I wouldn't do," Dillon added.

When Callum shot him a look, his younger brother laughed. "I'm giving you a wide berth of options."

"I think I can handle it," he murmured, flipping his

phone to silent mode. He slung the duffel over his shoulder and headed toward Becky.

She watched him approach, looking almost as wary as she did excited. "I hope you don't mind a little kidnapping," she said.

He cupped her cheeks between his palms and kissed her by way of an answer, ignoring the cheers and wolf whistles from his brothers.

"Are you sure about this?" he asked when they finally broke apart several minutes later. He smoothed the pads of his thumbs over her cheeks. "What about the girls?"

"Sarah and Grant are staying with them for the night," she answered, and he couldn't help but hear the catch in her voice.

"You don't have to leave them," he assured her. "I don't need a getaway, Becky. Any time we have together is special."

"I want this night," she said, her gaze sure and steady as she looked into his eyes. "If you do?"

"More than anything," he said and kissed her again.

They climbed into the car, and Becky pulled out onto the road that led to the highway.

"New ride?" Callum asked, grinning as she giggled at the Corvette's rapid acceleration.

"It's Grant's weekend car," she explained. "He inherited it from an uncle who lived in Florida. I guess he and Sarah don't drive it much around Rambling Rose, but he thought it would be more of a statement than picking you up in the minivan. I know it's not as fancy as the Audi, but—"

"You could pick me up on a bicycle, and I'd be happy."

"This is way more fun than a bike ride," she said with a wink.

He laughed. "That's true. Can I ask where we're headed?"

"Austin. We have reservations for dinner at a farm-to-table restaurant that has great reviews, and then a room at the Driskill. Your sister recommended the hotel, and the photos online look amazing."

"Everything about this is amazing," he told her without reservation.

After the doubts and worry that had been weighing on Callum's mind the past few days, being swept away for a romantic night in the city was the last thing he would have expected. Excitement zipped through him. He and Becky talked and laughed as she drove, and a heavy weight slowly lifted off his chest, replaced with an almost giddy lightness.

He could imagine how much it took for her to leave Sasha and Luna for the night, even with friends she trusted. It humbled him that she'd made that choice in order to spend more time with him.

The day was clear with the winter sun shining down on them like a bright omen. They arrived in Austin in the late afternoon and checked into the hotel located in the heart of downtown. Becky seemed enchanted by the Driskill's opulent lobby and the old-world charm of the decor. She insisted on giving her credit card to the front desk, and while Callum appreciated the gesture, he hoped he could convince her to allow him to pay for both dinner and the room. Just the fact that she'd arranged this evening meant the world to him.

He carried his duffel and her overnight bag to the room and watched with delight as Becky marveled over every understated but luxurious detail of the hotel. He liked seeing the world through her eyes. Despite all she'd been through, Becky still seemed able to appreciate the small joys.

"Oh, my gosh."

He was taking in the view from the room's wide window when she rushed out of the bathroom.

"There are three shower heads in one shower. I've only seen that on fancy home improvement shows."

Tenderness radiated through his heart and he pressed two fingers to his chest, unable to identify the feeling. Unwilling was more like it. He understood on some level that if he acknowledged the depth of his emotions toward this woman, they would change him in ways he couldn't handle at the moment.

So Callum did what he seemed to do best where Becky was concerned. He shoved down all the unfathomable feelings and concentrated on what was simple.

His need for her.

"We have some time before the dinner reservation." He made a show of looking at his watch as he walked toward her. "Just enough time by my calculations."

She bit down on her lower lip, sending a wave of lust rushing through him. "Enough time for what?"

"For the best shower of your life."

Her eyes went even darker. "You sound pretty confident about that."

"One thing I'm not lacking—" he nipped at the edge of her mouth "—is confidence in my ability to please you."

"That makes two of us," she said and led him into the hotel room's oversize bathroom.

* * *

"Can you zip me?" Becky asked, walking out of the bathroom later that evening.

Callum gave her an exaggerated ogle. "If I say no, can we get naked again and order room service for dinner?"

She rolled her eyes. "We've been naked pretty much since arriving in Austin," she reminded him.

"Best trip ever," he agreed.

The look in his dark eyes made her heart flutter. She never wanted that feeling to end, and somehow she knew with Callum it would last forever. Or at least as long as they had together. They'd had a magical afternoon, first in the shower and then moving to the bed. Part of her wanted to take him up on his half-joking offer. To spend the entire night wrapped in his arms.

But she gave a playful shake of her head and turned her back to him. "I've never been to Austin. We're hitting the town before we hit the sheets again."

"Whatever you want," he whispered, placing a gentle kiss on her exposed back before zipping up the dress. "You look beautiful tonight."

Becky drew in a deep breath as she glanced in the mirror that hung above the hotel room's cherry dresser. She felt beautiful. She'd bought the dress she wore, a silk sheath in a gorgeous blue, just before she found out she was pregnant. Only a few weeks prior to the accident that had claimed her husband's life.

When she went to pack for the trip early this morning, she'd found it shoved in the back of her closet, tags still intact.

Tears had pricked her eyes at the memory of those

dark days after Rick's death. She'd been desperate and overwhelmed, unsure of how she was supposed to manage her world without him. At that time, she hadn't even been able to imagine a moment when she'd feel as happy as she did right now.

Things weren't settled between her and Callum. She hadn't yet told him the three little words that could change everything. *I love you.* She wanted to wait for the right moment, but the longer she put it off the more significance the declaration seemed to take on in her mind and heart.

Still, the past few hours had bolstered her confidence. Callum seemed relaxed in a way that felt like a positive sign for the future. She couldn't imagine that he wouldn't return her feelings. Even if he wasn't ready to say the words back to her, she knew in her heart that he cared. Every thoughtful touch, every intense look made her know that she mattered to him.

As long as they were both willing to work at it, she believed they could overcome the pain of their individual pasts to build a shared future that would last a lifetime.

Chapter Fourteen

As they walked back to the Driskill later that night, Becky felt like she was floating on air, her feet barely touching the sidewalk.

"This night has been wonderful." They held hands, and his thumb grazing the pulse on her wrist made shivers track along her spine. "Austin is such a great city." She glanced up to the historic buildings they passed on their way to the hotel. "I can't believe how much of Texas I haven't seen when I've lived here all my life."

"Your parents didn't take you on many vacations?"

She shrugged, the mix of bitterness and affection she always felt when thinking of her parents settling over her like a blanket. At the moment, affection for them won out. It was difficult to feel anything but happy with her heart so full.

"My parents are simple people. They didn't feel like

they needed to travel, and money was always tight. My grandma and grandpa lived down on the coast, so I spent most summers with them. Even though I didn't go anywhere special, I never felt the lack of it growing up. I loved spending long days exploring the woods near their house and taking trips to the beach. Those memories are part of why we moved to Rambling Rose. I didn't want to raise my family in the city. Wide-open spaces are important."

"What about after you were married?" he asked quietly.

They were almost to the hotel, and she paused to enjoy the lights of the city. One day when they were older, she'd bring the girls here for a long weekend. They'd go to the zoo and the children's museum. She wanted to give them every experience she could so they'd understand life was an adventure. Hope burned in her like a flame that she and Callum might share that adventure.

It was strange to be thinking of that after he'd asked a question about her late husband. She wanted to believe Rick would be happy for her finding love again. He was that kind of man, and she knew he'd approve of Callum.

She glanced up at Callum, then straight ahead again. It was too difficult to share these deeply personal parts of herself while looking into his dark eyes. "Rick didn't talk about it, but he supported his mom financially from the time he graduated high school. His parents had divorced and his mom was an alcoholic, in and out of rehab. They weren't exactly close, but he loved her and wanted to take care of her." She took comfort in the steady pressure of Callum's hand holding hers.

"She was diagnosed with ovarian cancer after two

years of sobriety. Rick and I had just gotten married. We decided to postpone the honeymoon so that he could be with her through the surgery and treatments."

"He sounds like a wonderful son."

"He was a good man," she agreed. "His mom didn't have much in the way of health insurance, so there were a lot of doctor and hospital bills. We took care of as many of them as we could, but that meant there wasn't much money left over." That period ran through her mind like a movie. It had been stressful on Rick and on their marriage, but she would have never argued with his need to take care of his mother. "I guess my whole point is I haven't had a lot of opportunity for traveling."

"You can change that," he told her, lifting his free hand to tuck a lock of hair behind her ear.

"Oh, yes." She laughed. "One-year-old twins are really portable. There will be time for adventures. And I plan to take the girls on as many of them as I can manage."

With you at my side, she added silently. She should just say the words. Put them out there so that he knew how she felt.

But something held her back.

Callum wrapped his arms around her and pulled her close. "The more I learn about you, Becky, the more impressed I am at what a spectacular person you are."

"Anyone would do the same in my situation," she said automatically.

"I don't know about that." He kissed the top of her head. "I think you're special."

"Thanks," she whispered.

"Your late husband was a lucky man."

"I was the lucky one," she corrected, then pulled away to look at him. "I still am."

His jaw tensed for a split second before he flashed a smile. "We should get back to the hotel. It's late, and I have plans for you."

"For us." She lifted a hand to his face, smoothing her fingers over his stubbled jaw. "We're in this together."

"Together," he repeated softly.

Now, she told herself. *Tell him now.*

Her breath hitched and her mouth went dry. Why was saying she loved him so darn difficult? Was she truly so afraid of his reaction, or could it have more to do with the feeling of being disloyal to her late husband?

That thought made her stomach clench. She took Callum's hand and continued toward the hotel, hoping her sudden silence didn't tip him off to her emotions.

As difficult as it was to express how she felt, Becky had no trouble telling him everything she wanted to say with her body. Every time they came together, she learned more about both Callum and herself. And when she drifted off to sleep in his warm embrace, Becky couldn't help but believe everything would work out for the best.

The next morning, Becky and Callum checked out of the hotel and then walked to a popular breakfast spot a few blocks away. After filling up on omelets and stuffed French toast, they headed for a path near Lady Bird Lake. The temperatures hovered in the high fifties with low clouds on the horizon that meant they might be driving back to Rambling Rose in the rain.

A mother jogging behind a double stroller on the trail made her miss her girls. As lovely as the evening had been, she couldn't wait to get home and hug her babies. Sarah had FaceTimed her earlier, and the twins had smiled and blown kisses, bringing happy tears to Becky's eyes.

She felt refreshed but also anxious. She'd promised herself that before they left Austin to return to Rambling Rose, she'd talk to him about their future together.

"I hate for our getaway to end," Callum said with a charming grin. "I appreciate all the work you put into making last night special. It's going to be hard to top that as far as romance goes." He leaned in closer. "But I've got a few tricks up my sleeve."

She stopped walking and turned to fully face him. "I love you," she blurted.

He blinked and then blinked some more.

Becky opened her mouth, an apology ready to slip from her tongue. But no. She wasn't sorry. Even though Callum looked at her as if she'd just sprouted a second head, she didn't regret telling him how she felt. Maybe she could have done it with a bit more eloquence, but already she felt less nervous than she'd been since she'd decided she had to tell him.

"It's okay if you can't say it back to me." She offered what she hoped passed for an encouraging smile. "I don't want to rush things, but I needed to share that. You're an amazing man and these past few weeks have made me happier than I've been in a long time. I want it to continue. I want us to continue." The anxiety that had melted away for a moment began to reform, congealing in her belly like curdled milk. Something was wrong with Callum, and she couldn't bear to consider the reason for his reaction.

He continued to stare at her, then turned on his heel

and stalked several steps away. His shoulders went rigid with tension as he raked a stiff hand through his hair.

Something was very wrong.

"Callum." She moved toward him, reaching out a hand.

The moment she touched him, he recoiled, spinning to face her again.

"I'm leaving, Becky."

"Excuse me?" Her mind reeled. "I get it. We're both leaving this morning but—"

"Rambling Rose." He shook his head as if trying to shake his thoughts into some order. "Not for a while, at least not until the first round of projects opens. But after that…" He gave her an apologetic shrug. "I have to go."

"Why?" She breathed out the word on a ragged puff of air. "You love it in Rambling Rose." *I thought you loved me*, her heart screamed.

"I'm sorry," he said, sounding as miserable as she felt. "My business takes me all over the place. It's how things have always been."

"But they don't have to continue that way," she insisted. It wasn't like Becky to push. Normally she accepted whatever someone told her as fact and didn't argue or put up a fight. Her love for Callum made her a fighter. "I don't care if you travel. We can find a way to make it work. You and me together, Callum. I want—"

"That's just it." He started walking toward the street that led to the hotel, and she fell in step beside him, trying to make sense of what he was saying. "This isn't only about you and me. You have the girls to consider."

"They love you, too." As soon as the words were out of her mouth, she realized they were wrong. For a man clearly terrified of commitment, hearing that a pair of toddler twins cared about him might send him running even faster in the opposite direction.

"I don't want to hurt the girls or you."

"You already are," she told him, forcing herself to be honest. "I think you're hurting yourself the most. By believing the worst or that you're incapable of commitment or whatever bogus line you're telling yourself in your head and your heart. You're hurting all of us."

His step faltered as he glanced down on her, a pain so raw etched across his features it took her breath away. They'd come to the hotel's entrance, and she watched as couples, families and the hotel's efficient valet staff moved about. She thought she might have finally gotten through to Callum. Made it past whatever defenses he'd erected to avoid risking his heart.

But instead of uttering the words she longed to hear, he opened his mouth, then closed it again, shaking his head. "I'll get the car from the valet. I can drive home if you want."

"Sure," she whispered. *Home.* The word ricocheted around her mind like a bullet tearing through flesh. Callum had come to mean so much to her. He'd made her lonely little house feel like a home. But it had all been an illusion. No wonder she hadn't been able to express her feelings before now. Apparently, she should have trusted her preservation instincts.

Now she wanted to run and hide.

Instead, she wiped the emotion from her features and thanked the valet who opened the Corvette's passenger door for her. Everything about the past twenty-four hours seemed to mock her. The time she'd taken to set it up. Borrowing the car and making reservations.

The fact that she thought last night was a turning point in their relationship.

Turning it all to hell.

Callum climbed in behind the wheel and pulled out onto the downtown street. "Becky, I know—"

"You don't know anything," she said, working to keep her heartache in check. "I'm done talking for a while, Callum. I just want to go home and see my girls."

He gave a sharp nod, and a strained silence fell between them. Becky closed her eyes and let the sound of the engine lull her to sleep. As broken and rejected as she felt, somehow her body knew she needed a respite from the pain. It felt like only minutes passed, but the next time she opened her eyes they were pulling off the highway toward Rambling Rose.

"I guess I owe you an apology for keeping you awake most of last night," Callum said, flashing a sheepish smile. "You needed some extra sleep."

"I'm a single mother," she answered stonily, swiping a finger across the side of her mouth in case she'd drooled during her nap. "I always need sleep."

His smile faded. "I handled things badly this morning. I'm sorry. It's a huge honor to hear your feelings for me. I wish I could be the man to deserve your love."

"Seriously?" She took a deep breath. "Are you really going to give me the line about how 'it isn't you, it's me'? You're a good man, Callum. Everyone except you seems to realize it."

"I don't think I'm a bad guy," he said slowly as he pulled to a stop in the parking lot at The Shoppes, where the Fortune brothers had their modular office. "But I know I can't give you what you need."

Becky unbuckled her seat belt. "*Can't* and *won't* are two different things."

His eyes widened slightly.

She still wasn't ready to play nice when so much was on the line. She'd loved and lost once before. The tragedy and sorrow of her husband's accident had brought her to her knees, literally and figuratively. It had taken a long time for her to manage to get up on her feet again. As much as her heart hurt, she wouldn't let herself fall back down again.

"I'm sorry," he repeated. "This doesn't mean things have to end between us right now. I'm leaving tomorrow on a scouting trip to San Antonio for a couple of days but when I get back—"

"San Antonio?" She turned to face him. "So you already have a plan for where you're moving next?"

"Not exactly a plan, but Fortune Brothers Construction has a few irons in the fire."

She swallowed against the bile rising in her throat. He'd known all this time he was leaving. She shouldn't be surprised. Callum hadn't made promises to her. Yet how could she have misread the situation so completely?

"It would be better if we ended this now," she managed, not bothering to worry that a tiny sob slipped out along with the words. She dabbed at the corners of her eyes. "I need to think about the future for myself and my girls. If you aren't going to be a part of it, there's no point in continuing."

"I care about you, Becky."

"It's not enough." Before he could answer, she got out of the car and slammed shut the passenger door. She was too close to losing it to continue this conversation. Besides, what was left to say?

She couldn't stand for him to try to convince her they could continue until he finally left Rambling Rose. Her daughters already had a special connection with him. A few more months would only make it harder when he left for good. Not to mention what it would do to Becky.

A clean break now was the right decision even though her heart screamed in protest.

He got out of the car as she walked around the front.

"Things don't have to end this way," he said, moving to stand in front of her.

She forced herself to look up at him. "Things don't have to end at all, but you're too afraid of being hurt to commit to anything." She drew in a ragged breath. "You're too much of coward to even try."

He seemed to freeze at her words, and she elbowed her way past him and into the car. With shaking fingers, she gripped the steering wheel with one hand and the gearshift in the other. She put the car into Drive and roared out of the parking lot, leaving a cloud of dust and Callum Fortune behind.

Chapter Fifteen

Callum threw himself into work for the next several days, refusing to discuss Becky or their breakup with Stephanie or either of his brothers.

He told himself the situation was his personal business, but in truth he didn't want or need his siblings to point out how he'd behaved like an idiot. Not when he was handling that so effectively on his own.

How could he have been so happy and then ruin it on purpose? He barely understood why he'd made the choice to tell her he planned to leave Rambling Rose.

Up until that instant, he hadn't decided anything for certain. Hell, he hadn't actually scheduled a visit to potential investment properties near San Antonio, although he needed to come up with a plan for where his company could do the most good.

Too bad that the thought of leaving held no appeal.

He'd dropped that little bomb in the aftermath of those three tiny words she'd shared with him. Any man would be lucky to be loved by a woman like Becky. Callum knew that without a doubt.

Unfortunately, he also believed that eventually—whether he meant to or not—he'd hurt her. His short-lived marriage had taught him that he simply didn't have the capacity for love a man needed to keep a woman happy. He was a man who needed independence. He'd already given everything he could and had nothing left.

Becky might want to believe he was worthy of her, but Callum knew better. He rolled his shoulders as he stared at his computer monitor, trying to shrug off some of the tension that had rooted there like one of the ranch's decades-old oak trees.

Whenever he wasn't on-site, he was, like today, at his desk in the Fortune Brothers Construction office near The Shoppes. There were so many aspects of the business to manage, especially now that the triplets had jumped headfirst into designing the restaurant. Ashley, Megan and Nicole were planning to visit Rambling Rose at the end of the month, and Callum wanted to make their trip a productive one. The breadth of projects they'd taken on in this town were the most expansive of his career.

He'd also never felt so connected to a place as he did to this small town. His father had worried about them moving to Texas and the possible influence of the extended Fortune family. The kidnapping that had occurred at last year's wedding of Callum's uncle Gerald had shaken David, making him wary of deepening his branch's ties to the rest of the Fortunes. Callum hadn't given it much thought. Before now, the locations he'd chosen for his projects had been based solely on the historic value and financial prospects.

Rambling Rose was proving to be different, and not just because of Becky. Maybe it was the history the Fortune family played in the town. It still gave Callum goose bumps to think about the pediatric center, their first major project, being built on the site of the Fortune's Foundling Hospital. Linus also had a link to that piece of history, given that his mother had purposely left him at the site of the former Fortune orphanage.

If he didn't know better, he'd swear he could feel the spirit of this community trickling into him, changing who he was at a cellular level. It was a ridiculous thought, of course, brought on by the lack of sleep and missing Becky.

A million times since that drive home from Austin, he'd wanted to call her. He hated how they'd left things, what she must think of him. He hated that he couldn't be the man she wanted.

"Is this an okay time for a break?"

A smile broke over his face as his stepmom walked into the office. For the first time since Becky drove away in her red Corvette, he took a full breath. Marci wore beige slacks and a cashmere sweater, not a hair out of place as she grinned at him.

"This is the best surprise I could imagine," he told her, standing and walking around the desk to wrap her in a tight hug.

Marci smelled like lilacs and vanilla, two scents he'd always associate with home. "Stephanie said she didn't need help," his stepmom explained, placing a quick kiss on his cheek. "But that baby is such a cute little guy. I couldn't resist an opportunity to love on him."

"We're all so proud of her. Everyone is still holding out hope that Linus's mother returns, but there's no better place for him than with Stephanie."

Marci's smile turned wistful. "You were such troupers when the triplets were born. I know you took on the lion's share of the responsibility for them when I needed help."

"It wasn't a big deal." He didn't like discussing that time with anyone in his family because the lingering resentment he harbored made him feel like a jerk. He loved the triplets and the rest of his family. It had been his choice to step up when Marci needed help. No one had forced him. He'd simply done what he had to for his family.

"All that responsibility took a toll on you," she said softly.

There was no point bothering to deny it. Not with his perceptive stepmom. "Would you like to see some of the projects we're working on?" he asked instead. "We can start right here at The Shoppes."

She studied him for a moment, clearly understanding a distraction when one was shoved at her. "I'd love that."

Callum breathed a sigh of relief as he led her from the office. "Have you seen Steven and Dillon?"

"Not yet. I flew into Houston last night and drove over to Rambling Rose this morning. I called Stephanie on my way into town and met her at the pediatric center so that I could visit Linus at day care. Then I came here."

"Steven had a meeting about the hotel, but then he was due back here so we could go over some paint samples with the designer. Dillon is probably at the spa or the vet clinic."

"It feels like you're so busy," Marci said, and he heard the pride in her voice. "I can't believe how much you've taken on in such a short time."

"I like to be busy." Callum laughed softly. "But we both know Fortune Brothers Construction wouldn't be half as successful without Steven and Dillon in the mix. The three of us together bring the magic."

"You've always had a soft spot for your brothers and sisters." Marci reached across the console and patted his arm. "I can't help but worry about what that's cost you."

They walked from the modular office toward the entrance of The Shoppes at Rambling Rose. The building had housed an old five-and-dime, but they'd taken it nearly down to the studs to rebuild it into an upscale set of shops that ultimately would include fashion, jewelry and a designer home accessory store. Their neighbors in Rambling Rose Estates seemed especially excited about this upcoming addition to the community, although Dillon still worried locals weren't totally on board with the plan.

He didn't give much credence to that. Every one of his projects had received a bit of pushback in the initial stages. He believed beyond a doubt they were improving this town for everyone, and Callum hoped that as the longtime residents began to patronize the new businesses they'd realize the changes benefited everyone.

"I have a great life that's even better because of how close we all are. Although it's going to be interesting when the triplets arrive. I'm not sure Rambling Rose has ever seen anything like the three of them on a mission."

"If anyone can help ease the transition for the girls, it's you." Marci stopped and shook her head. "I'm sorry,

Callum. That's the problem. We all assume you'll help with whatever someone in the family needs."

"I will," he answered without hesitation.

"But you shouldn't have to," she told him gently. "It's past time we allow you to put your life first. The family you create for yourself with your own—"

"No." He held up a hand. "I tried going down that path and failed. I'm not going to have a family of my own. My independence means too much to me."

"You and Doralee weren't a good match. That doesn't mean you have to give up on love completely. What about that nurse and her adorable twins from the ribbon-cutting ceremony? Stephanie told me you've been spending a lot of time with her."

"Stephanie shares too much," he said and started walking toward the building again. He waved to a few guys on the crew as Marci caught up to him.

"Don't get snippy. Your sister wouldn't have to keep me apprised of what's going on in your life if you'd tell me yourself."

"Becky and I are over," he said simply. "She doesn't want to waste time on a guy who's a bad bet for the future."

"You are not a bad bet," his stepmom insisted, sounding affronted that he'd dare utter those words.

"I love you," he said, giving her shoulder a quick squeeze. "But I'm not ready to talk about it."

"I'm here when you are," she answered.

Steven caught sight of them at that moment and strode over with a wide grin, catching Marci in a big bear hug.

The pain in Callum's chest eased slightly as he spent the rest of the workday with his brothers and stepmom.

After a quick tour of the progress on The Shoppes, they caught up with Dillon at the planned spa location. Like the devoted mother she was, Marci oohed and aahed at all the improvements they were making in town.

They took her to lunch at the Mexican restaurant where he'd eaten with Becky and the girls, and then they headed toward the old feed and grain building that would be the triplets' restaurant.

"The three of them have been able to talk about little else since you put the wheels in motion on this project," Marci confided as she spun in a slow circle to take in the space. "It's really exciting."

"We're staging a Texas takeover," Dillon said with a laugh.

Marci arched a brow. "You're a few decades behind the curve on that. Fortunes have been making their mark in Texas forever, it seems."

"But this place is ours," Steven clarified. "I know the Fortunes have longstanding ties here as well, and maybe that's why Rambling Rose feels like home."

Callum's chest ached at his brother's words. A significant part of why the town felt like home to him was Becky. Even though not speaking to her over the past few days had been horrible, he could still feel their connection. She might hate him at the moment, but just knowing she was nearby gave him some comfort.

Of course, it also motivated him to ensure the current slate of projects stayed on schedule so there'd be nothing to prevent him from moving on. Surely some other man would swoop in and capture Becky's heart. Though it might actually kill Callum to see her with someone else.

"You look so sad," Marci told him quietly as Dillon

and Steve launched into a discussion about how many treatment rooms they'd need.

"I wish Dad wanted to spend more time in Texas," he told his stepmom when her perceptive gaze landed on him. Let Marci think his inner turmoil centered on that and not Becky.

"He worries about all of you and wants you to be safe."

"We are."

"I know." She offered a gentle smile. "He'll come around. He was so proud of you at the opening of the pediatric center, and he's excited to see the vet clinic, especially since Stephanie will be working there." Marci checked her watch. "Which reminds me, she's picking up Linus in a few minutes and I promised I'd be at the ranch when they arrived."

"We can head back to the office to get your car."

They said goodbye to Dillon and Steven, both of whom would be joining them for a big family dinner at the house later. If Becky hadn't ended things, she and her girls would have been invited, too. He knew Marci would have been thrilled to have three babies to love on.

He didn't mention it, but he missed Becky more than he could say. How many times would he have to remind himself the breakup was for the best before he believed it?

Becky drove out to the ranch the following afternoon, her stomach fluttering with nerves.

To her surprise, the surly young man who'd given her so much trouble when she'd approached the gate the last time waved her through with a smile on this occasion.

She should feel vindicated, but it had been difficult

to muster any kind of happiness ever since she'd said goodbye to Callum.

Stephanie had texted and asked her to visit baby Linus. Callum's sister hadn't directly referenced the breakup, but she'd made a point in the text of telling Becky that Callum wouldn't be home.

Maybe Becky should have said no. Cutting off ties with anyone named Fortune was probably best. But she wanted to see the baby and considered Stephanie a friend. She hadn't just lost a boyfriend when she ended things with Callum. The Fortunes had made her feel so welcome, and she'd soaked up their generosity and friendship like she was a sponge left out in the rain.

"Cawl," Luna shouted as they pulled up to the house. How had she remembered?

Sasha popped the binky out of her mouth. "Cawl."

Blinking away tears, Becky unbuckled her seat belt and turned to face her daughters. "Callum's not here right now, but we're going to see baby Linus and Miss Stephanie."

"Gog," Sasha whispered.

"Yes." Becky smiled at her sweet girl. "I'm sure we'll get to see the animals, too."

She got the girls out of the minivan and carried them toward the front door. Before she could knock, it opened to reveal Marci Fortune, Callum's elegant stepmother.

"Hi," Becky breathed, her hold on the twins tightening.

"Hello, Becky." Marci gave her a disarmingly friendly smile. "It's nice to see you again. Please come in. May I hold one of your sweet girls?"

"Sure."

As soon as Marci held out her hands, Luna reached

for her. Sasha rested her head on Becky's shoulder, watching her sister as she sucked on her beloved binky.

"Stephanie didn't mention you were visiting," Becky said, then blushed at the thought that Marci must know about her breakup with Callum. He'd told her that Marci was protective of her children, even as adults, and wondered what the older woman thought.

Probably that Becky was the biggest idiot alive to reject her handsome, wealthy, charming stepson.

"My daughter appreciates all the help you've given her with the baby," Marci said as she led Becky through the house toward the wing that Stephanie occupied. "She tells me you've been invaluable sharing your expertise and offering support."

"It's a wonderful thing she's doing with Linus," Becky answered honestly. "Obviously she had a great role model because her maternal instincts are spot-on." She cleared her throat, then added, "I'm still holding out hope that Laurel returns to claim her baby. We talked a bit that first day she came to the pediatric center. Who knows how much she remembers of the things she told me, but it was clear she had a lot of love to give. I don't know what happened to push her to the point of relinquishing Linus."

"Becoming a mother isn't always as easy as people want you to believe," Marci said with a sigh. "I struggled with my health, both physical and mental, after the triplets. Even before when we were trying for more children." Her eyes gleamed with unshed tears. "I'm sure Callum shared with you how much responsibility he took on during that time."

"I know he loves you and his sisters very much."

"That's kind of you to say, but it took a toll on him. I

didn't realize how large of one until recently. He cares about you, Becky. You and your girls." She bounced Luna gently in her arms.

Becky nodded. "But he's planning to leave Rambling Rose. My life is here, and I can't have someone become close to the girls who isn't going to be a part of their lives long-term. It's not fair to them."

"I understand." Marci reached out to stroke a finger across Sasha's cheek. "They're precious. My hope would be that he changes his mind and you give him another chance."

Becky closed her eyes as she considered that possibility. Would she give him another chance? She almost laughed at the absurdity of the question. Callum could have a thousand chances if that's what it took.

"Mom." Stephanie appeared in the doorway, the baby wrapped in a blue blanket and cradled in her arms. "Stop hogging Becky. I want her to see Linus before he falls asleep again."

"I think he's gotten bigger already," Becky exclaimed as she walked to her friend, and Stephanie beamed in response. "Hey, buddy."

Her girls babbled at little Linus and they all headed for the sitting room Stephanie had set up with a play mat, bounce seat and motorized swing.

They visited while her girls played with the baby's toys, largely entertained by Marci. Stephanie had a list of questions about the infant's care and specific milestones that Becky was happy to answer.

Neither Stephanie nor her mom brought up Callum again, which was both a relief and a disappointment. She wasn't sure she could handle talking about him, but wanted so badly to ask how he was doing.

Was he as miserable as she?

After almost an hour of wakefulness, Linus fell asleep in Stephanie's arms. She transferred him to her mother and walked Becky and the twins to the front door.

"Thanks for coming over," she said. "I hope it wasn't too weird with how things stand between you and Callum."

"Actually, it wasn't," Becky said, surprised to find the statement to be true. She buckled Sasha and Luna into their car seats and then turned to Stephanie. "Even though things ended with your brother, I hope we can still be friends."

"Me, too," Stephanie said. "You might be the first real friend I've made in Rambling Rose. At least the only one who doesn't think I'm crazy for becoming a foster parent."

"They must not realize how big of a heart you have."

Stephanie leaned forward and gave Becky a hug. "Thank you," she whispered, then added, "I'm sorry my brother's a big dummy."

A laugh popped out of Becky's mouth. "He's a good man," she corrected. "He just needs to realize it."

After another squeeze, Stephanie released her and Becky climbed into the minivan and headed home. The sun had started to set across the western sky, leaving trails of pink and orange in its wake. A glance in the rearview mirror showed that her girls were staring out at the beauty of the sky, and their wide-eyed wonder made Becky smile.

She didn't know if it was possible that she and Callum might get another chance, but the conversation with his sister had given her a bit of hope.

Hope that turned to dust in her throat as she approached the entrance gatehouse. A large silver truck, which she immediately recognized as Callum's, pulled through the gate.

Becky's heart hammered in her chest as their gazes met. Then she realized he wasn't alone. In the passenger seat sat a beautiful blonde. It was difficult to get a good look at the woman as she drove past, but Becky could tell she was young and strikingly gorgeous.

Swallowing hard, she turned her attention back to the road and tried not to cry. The moment was over in seconds, but the meaning of it lashed her like the sting of a whip.

Callum had moved on. His sister and stepmom might claim he still cared about Becky, but how much could she have meant to him if he was already on a date and bringing the woman home?

Becky hadn't realized it was possible for her heart to break any more until it splintered into a million pieces.

Chapter Sixteen

"I thought you were going to try to get home early last night."

"Good morning to you, too," Callum told his step-mom as she walked into the kitchen early the next morning. He'd expected to be gone by the time anyone else in the family woke, but should have known Marci wouldn't let him off the hook so easily.

"Good morning," she said with a smile. She joined him at the counter. He handed her a mug from the cabinet and then watched as she filled it with the coffee he'd just brewed. "Did I misunderstand the plan?"

Frustration wove its way through his veins like a needle and thread. He'd planned to return home before Becky left, hoping he'd get a chance to talk to her. He missed her so badly it felt like he'd lost part of his heart without her in his life. "I got sidetracked by a neighbor's daughter. She's home from college for the weekend and her car broke down in town. I helped her get it to the mechanic, then gave her a ride home." He rolled his shoulders. "Becky was just pulling through the main gate when I drove in."

"She's lovely, Callum. Not just her looks, either, although she's quite pretty."

"Beautiful," he countered softly.

Marci inclined her head. "Beautiful. Yes. But I got a sense of her kindness and strength yesterday. Her daughters adore her and she patiently answers every one of Stephanie's questions and seems so interested in Linus's welfare, even after a full day at work. I could tell she's a truly good person."

"Is this supposed to make me feel better?" He pushed out a laugh to soften the question when his tone came out harsher than he'd meant it. "I know I messed up with a one-in-a-million woman. But there's nothing—"

"You can fight for her," his stepmother interrupted.

"I've texted to check in with her every day since she ended things. She never replies."

"Your generation and those infernal devices." Marci sniffed. "You don't win a woman back with a text. Be bold, Callum. Give her a reason to try again."

"I'm afraid I don't have one," he admitted, pressing the heels of his palms to his closed eyes. "I'm not willing to risk my heart. She was right about me."

"What makes you think that?" Marci asked. "Your divorce?"

He dropped his hands to his sides and forced himself to meet his stepmother's concerned gaze. "I failed at marriage once, and it about killed me to hurt Doralee that way."

"She wasn't right for you from the start."

Both he and Marci turned as Stephanie joined them in the kitchen, a sleeping Linus cradled in her arms.

"I'm not sure I can take being double-teamed by the two of you," he told his sister.

Stephanie rolled her eyes. "Be an awesome brother and pour me a cup of coffee. This little guy was up more than normal last night. I'm dragging right now."

"I'll take him," Marci offered, setting down her coffee. "While you talk some sense into your brother." She smiled when Callum narrowed his eyes. "I'm stepping back so you don't feel like we're ganging up on you. But know I agree with everything Stephanie says."

His sister handed the baby to Marci, then faced Callum. "You're an idiot," she said simply.

Callum snorted. "What happened to the family rule of no name-calling in front of Mom?"

"It's not exactly how I would have put it," Marci admitted, "but she has a point."

"You know it, too." Stephanie accepted the cup of coffee he offered, sighing as she took a long drink. "You love Becky Averill and her daughters and you want to make a life with them." She pointed a finger toward him. "In Rambling Rose."

He shook his head. "I don't—"

"This is your home," Stephanie interrupted. "And Becky is your person. Stop trying to deny it."

"She broke up with me," he pointed out, his heart twisting painfully in his chest.

"From what I gather, you left her no choice." She leaned in closer. "I tried to get her to talk bad about you last night. I really did. And she wouldn't do it. She loves you and if you'd just get out of your own way, you could have the life we all know you want."

Marci joined her daughter. "I told you I'd agree with everything she said. We all know how much you sacrificed for this family and how the divorce made you question things. But you're a family man at heart, Callum. You always have been."

He opened his mouth to argue, then paused and drew in a deep breath instead. He'd spent a lot of years convincing himself he didn't want the responsibility of that kind of commitment.

Now he couldn't imagine his life without Becky and the girls in it. He hadn't expected his life to take this turn, but his sister was right, as usual. He'd be an idiot not to risk his heart when he had this chance at real happiness. And yet...

"I can't compete with her late husband," he said quietly, finally voicing his greatest fear when it came to Becky. "From all accounts, he was damn near a saint. The perfect husband who would have been a perfect father."

"Callum." Stephanie squeezed his arm. "I promise you that Becky isn't looking for perfect. Her girls don't need that, either. They just need someone to love them."

"I do," he whispered. "I will if she'll let me." Allowing himself to acknowledge that undeniable fact lifted the weight that had been crushing his chest.

His stepmom and sister shared a smile. "Then don't you think it's time you shared that with Becky?"

He gave them each a quick hug, dropped a kiss on the top of baby Linus's downy head and quickly headed for his truck.

Becky would be at work by now, so he drove straight

to the pediatric center, trying to work out a plan in his mind for how to win her back.

The best he could think of past his racing heart and sweaty palms was throwing himself to his knees and begging her for another chance.

Surely something better would present itself in the moment, but either way Callum wasn't going to let anything stop him.

He rushed through the lobby and down the hall that housed the primary care wing.

Becky's friend Sharla sat at the nurses' station, giving him a look that could freeze the sun as he approached.

"I need to speak with Becky," he said, forcing a calm tone.

"She's not here."

He glanced around as if he could will her to appear. "When will she be back?"

"Dunno."

Okay, this wasn't going the way he'd planned, but if his bid for another chance with Becky needed to include groveling to her coworker, he'd do that.

"I've been an idiot," he told the surly medical assistant. He figured if his sister had been willing to tell him that out loud, most people in Becky's life must agree.

"Go on," Sharla said slowly, proving him right.

"She's the best thing that ever happened to me, and I'm sorry I hurt her."

"You hurt her badly."

He sucked in a breath. "I want to make it up to her and the twins. I can't lose them. They're my world."

The woman studied him for several long moments

before nodding. "I actually believe you… But she still isn't here."

He sighed. Damn. "When will she be back?"

"Two days." Sharla tapped a finger against her chin. "Maybe three. If she doesn't decide—"

"Decide what?" Callum's mind reeled. "Where did she go? She left Rambling Rose? That's impossible. This is her home."

"Slow down, cowboy." Sharla stood and placed her palms on the desk. "I believe you love our Becky, but that doesn't mean I'm convinced you're what's best for her. Especially after she saw you bringing home another woman."

Callum felt his mouth go slack. "What woma—" He muttered a curse. "Last night when I passed her at the gatehouse? I wasn't on a date or bringing anyone home. I'd wanted to get to the ranch before Becky left, but I had to give my neighbor's daughter a lift home when her car broke down in town."

Sharla's pink-glossed lips formed a small O.

"Please don't tell me Becky left town thinking I was already dating someone else."

"I won't tell you." Sharla made a face. "Which doesn't make it any less of a fact."

"I have to talk to her."

A patient came out of one of the exam rooms with Parker, who lifted a questioning brow in Callum's direction.

"I might have fibbed about her return date," Sharla said quickly. "I need to get back to work, but she went to see her parents in Houston. She's planning on coming home tomorrow night. Talk to her then and you better make it good. Becky deserves the best you've got, Mr. Fortune."

"She deserves the best of everything," he agreed. He just hoped he could convince her a second chance was best for both of them.

Becky blinked away tears as she watched her mother place a kiss on Sasha's chubby cheek. The quieter twin sat in her mom's lap while Luna grinned and banged a wooden spoon on the colorful xylophone that had been Becky's as a child.

"I can't believe you saved all these toys," she told her mom.

Ann Averill shrugged. "They were your favorites, so I figured if you had kids one day they'd like them, too."

"The girls are in heaven."

It wasn't just the twins, either. A sense of peace had descended over Becky as she'd relaxed in her childhood home. Despite how they'd acted toward her in the past, she wished she hadn't waited so long to reach out.

A twinge of sorrow pinched her chest as memories of the weeks after Rick's death filled her mind. She'd been overwhelmed by grief, which had quickly morphed into anger when her parents tried to convince her to move home to Houston.

She'd felt their lack of confidence that she could make it on her own in Rambling Rose like a slap in the face. Her pain had made her even more determined to manage life on her own without asking for help. They'd never been a particularly close family, and the rift had seemed to widen on its own until it had been easier not to speak to them at all than to listen to her mother's subtle digs or her father's outright condemnation.

Spending time with the Fortunes had reminded her of the importance of family. Her relationship with her parents might not be perfect, but she wanted her daughters to know their grandma and grandpa.

"They look like your grandmother," her mom said, her gaze wistful as she snuggled Sasha and smiled at Luna. "I thought the same about you when you were a baby."

Becky nodded. "And they have Rick's smile," she whispered.

"You're a good mom, Beck." Becky glanced up to where her father stood in the doorway, a spatula in hand. Her dad grilled all year round and had started prepping the steaks almost as soon as Becky and the twins had arrived that morning.

Tom Averill was a gruff man, quiet and solid, and he'd always communicated his affection through action rather than words. Some of the best memories Becky had from her childhood were of her father flipping pancakes while Becky watched Saturday morning cartoons at the kitchen counter.

"Thanks, Dad." Becky managed the words without crying, which she knew would embarrass her stoic father.

He gave a curt nod and disappeared again.

"He's proud of you," her mother said. "We both are."

"Really?" Becky laughed. "I had the impression you thought I was in over my head."

"Perhaps at the time of Rick's death," her mother admitted. "We were so worried about you recovering from that kind of tragedy. Then when you found out you were carrying twins…" Ann shook her head. "I didn't believe in you as much as I should. You're much stronger than either your father or I realized."

"You raised me," Becky said softly, "so you can take some of the credit."

Her mother chuckled. "No. You get it all." Her expression sobered. "I still worry about you and wish you'd move home. The girls need—"

"Rambling Rose is our home, Mom." Becky smiled and clapped along with Luna's enthusiastic banging. "We're part of the community." Her breath hitched as she realized how true that statement was. She owed a large debt to Callum for helping her finally muster the courage to come out of her shell. Because of the way she was raised, she'd thought of asking for help as a weakness.

Rick had been equally independent and their relationship had been the two of them against the world. It worked until his death, and then she was lost at sea with not even a paddle to aid her in getting to dry land.

From the first moment Callum had volunteered to watch the twins while she helped Laurel, he'd made it easy to lean on him. She'd gotten close to the people at work in a way she hadn't before and begun to expand her circle of friends, enriching both her life and the twins'.

Would she have been willing to make that happen without Callum's innate support? Hard to say, but Becky would remain forever grateful to him.

Her feelings about Callum must have shown on her face because her mother's expression became suddenly assessing.

"Have you met someone new?" Ann asked as she smoothed a hand over Sasha's back.

"I went on a few dates with a guy, but it didn't work out."

"Why?"

"We wanted different things, I guess." Becky picked an invisible piece of lint from her pant leg. "He's not sure if he's going to stay in Rambling Rose long-term, and my life is there."

"Is it?" Her mother sounded more curious than judgmental. "You're a nurse, Beck. You can have a career anywhere. The girls are so young that a move wouldn't really impact them. There's something about how you look right now that makes me think this man was special to you."

Becky drew in a sharp breath, and her mother sighed. "We might not have the closest relationship," Ann said, "but I'm still your mom. I know you, sweetheart."

"I can't leave my home," Becky said, her voice cracking on the last word. She cleared her throat. "Rick and I chose Rambling Rose. Even if I wanted to relocate, I don't know how I could. It would feel like I was being disloyal to his memory. Like I was moving on."

"No," her mother answered immediately. "That isn't true."

Sasha climbed off her grandma's lap, as if sensing Becky's distress, and toddled toward her, Luna quickly following suit.

Becky opened her arms and cradled her twins. "People tell me that," she said to Ann. "They tell me it's okay to move on. But I don't want to *move on*. Rick will always be a part of me. He's a part of our beautiful daughters. His death made me who I am today."

"I understand." Her mother nodded. "Which is why I don't believe you have to stay in Rambling Rose. It's fine if you want to. I'm not trying to convince you to leave. But if you meet someone who makes you and the girls happy, that's important. Rick would want you to be happy again. You can honor him by living life to the fullest."

Was she doing the opposite now? Yes, she felt a connection to Rambling Rose. The town was her home. But it didn't compare with how happy she'd been with Callum. She didn't know if he'd even consider the option of Becky and the girls going with him when he left. But she knew his fear of staying in one place wasn't about her. They could make a life together wherever the work took him if that's what he needed. She understood his fear about settling down, but she could show him that the home they both craved wasn't simply a matter of four walls. It was in their connection to each other. Had she given up too easily? Had her doubts and fears about what she had to offer led her to make the biggest mistake of her life?

Callum's heart beat double time as he drove past the park on the edge of town and saw Becky's minivan parked in the gravel lot.

Sharla had texted him that Becky was definitely coming to work the following morning so his plan had been to talk to her after her shift tomorrow night.

He could still do that, he thought, as nerves thrummed through his veins. Chances were she'd gotten back recently and probably wanted some time to decompress after the visit with her parents.

Excuses. He had a million of them.

None could mask the fact that he was afraid Becky wouldn't give him a second chance. That he'd put his heart on the line and have it well and truly broken. His ex-wife hadn't been the only one hurt when their marriage ended. It had taken a while for Callum to admit it, but he still carried the scars from his divorce.

He'd been a less than perfect husband and didn't want to ever fail in that way again. But now he realized if he continued to guard his heart so tightly that there wasn't room for anyone inside it, he might protect himself from pain but he'd also prevent himself from finding true happiness.

The kind he knew he'd have with Becky.

Before he changed his mind, Callum pulled into the parking lot and stopped next to her vehicle, refusing to waste one more minute on doubt and regret. It was close to sundown, but the air was calm and the lingering scent of an earlier rain shower made everything earthy and fresh.

He passed a few people walking dogs or jogging on the path as he walked toward the bench overlooking a small pond where he knew he'd find Becky and the girls.

His hand strayed to the side pocket of his cargo pants and the outline of the black velvet box he'd carried around with him since that morning.

She seemed lost in thought as he approached, her lips moving as if she were talking to her daughters or maybe to her late husband. She'd shared that this was the place she felt closest to Rick, and suddenly Callum felt like an interloper, intruding in a moment where he didn't belong.

Then Luna, who was leaning forward in the double stroller, spotted him.

"Cawl," she cried, then shoved a piece of oat cereal into her mouth and lifted her arms toward him.

Sasha pulled the binky out of her mouth to call out to him as well, and Becky met his gaze with a gasp.

"I hope you don't mind company," he said as he got closer.

"No," she whispered and offered a tentative smile.

The girls bounced and clapped and reached for him, like two little baby birds in the nest. "Is it okay if I pick them up?"

"Of course." Her fingers clasped and released the hem of her faded sweatshirt over and over. Apparently, he wasn't the only one with a case of nerves.

He unbuckled the girls, lifted them into his arms and then sat next to Becky on the bench.

"I heard you went to visit your parents," he said as Sasha snuggled into him and Luna patted his cheek. He'd missed not only Becky this week, but her girls, as well. His heart stammered at the thought of getting another chance to be in their lives, hopefully on a permanent basis.

"Just for a night," she confirmed, then frowned. "How did you hear?"

"I stopped by the pediatric center yesterday."

"Oh."

"To see you."

"I gathered that," she said with a slight smile.

"You haven't returned my texts."

Her gaze softened. "I thought a clean break between us would be easier."

"Right," he muttered. "And now here I am intruding on your evening walk."

"It's okay, Callum. I'm glad to see you."

Hope had never played a huge role in his life, but now he grabbed on to the kernel of it, holding it close to his heart like a lifeline. "Were you visiting with Rick?" he forced himself to ask.

"I know it seems silly, but yes. I wanted to talk to him after being with my parents and this is the spot where I come for that."

"Is anything the matter with your folks?"

She shook her head. "It had been too long since I've seen them. I want the twins to know their family." She reached out a hand and squeezed his arm. "The Fortunes have inspired me, actually. It's great how close all of you are, even when you live halfway across the country from each other."

"Family is a gift." He kissed the top of Sasha's head. "Until they drive you crazy."

"Yeah." She laughed and lifted Luna from his arms. "It was good to see the girls with their grandparents. Hard to tell if we'll be able to put everything in the past behind us, but I'm glad I made the effort. My mom actually had some great advice about my future."

A momentary flicker of panic gripped his gut. "Tell me you aren't moving away from Rambling Rose."

"No plans for that at the moment." She adjusted her hold on Luna. "Although Mom doesn't understand my devotion to this town, and what she said made a lot of sense."

"It's your home," he argued, not wanting Becky to compromise her commitment for anyone. "Rambling Rose is the place you and Rick chose to build a life. Of course you're dedicated to this town."

She studied him for a moment. "Believe it or not," she said, "she wasn't judging me. That's what I'd always thought about my parents. I think they're glad that I'm happy here, but they also want me to know I could make a home anywhere. Rick will always be with me."

"And with your girls. His love is a part of all three of you."

"Exactly." She swiped at her cheek. "You understand."

"I hope *you* understand that I'd never try to take his place." Callum swallowed. Hard. "But I love you, Becky. I should have told you before now, and I'm sorry I hurt you. You were right to call me a coward. You make me want to be brave. I'd do anything for another chance. I promise I won't mess it up again."

"I love you, too," she whispered. "I never want you to think that this town—that anyplace—is more important to me than you."

He lifted a finger to her lips. "It's your home, and it's my home, too. I want to build a life here with you." He hugged Sasha closer. "With the girls. They will never forget their father, but it would be my great honor to raise them and be as much of a dad as I can be."

"Do you mean that?" She sniffed and the tenderness in her gaze made his heart melt all over again. "I know you've had enough of a burden with taking care of little ones and that—"

"It would never be a burden," he corrected. "Being a part of the twins' lives would be the best thing that I could imagine."

He fished in his pocket for the velvet box. "In fact…"

Becky's dark eyes widened.

"I hope you'll excuse me if I don't get down on one knee," he said with a chuckle. "Sasha seems to have fallen asleep on my shoulder and I don't want to disturb her."

"No knee necessary," she whispered.

"Becky Averill." He flipped open the box to reveal the ring he'd chosen at the jeweler's that morning. It was a round diamond set in a platinum band with two smaller stones flanking the one in the center. "Would you be my wife? I promise to never give up on our love and to spend the rest of my life making you happy."

Luna cooed out her approval of the ring as she grabbed at it. Becky held her daughter out of reach, then met Callum's gaze. "Yes," she told him and it felt like a symphony swelled in his chest.

"There's something else." He set the box on the bench and reached in his opposite pocket, taking out a small velvet pouch and handing it to Becky. "I got these for the girls."

She pulled out the two gold bracelets he'd also chosen at the jewelers. "I love you, Becky," he repeated. "And I love your daughters. This is my way of telling you that my heart belongs to all three of you." He shook his head. "You're crying. Don't cry."

"They're happy tears," she promised, her voice catching on the last word. "But you better put that ring onto my finger now. I'm not sure I can wait any longer."

"Then let's not wait," he said, plucking the ring from the box and slipping it onto her left hand. "I want us to be a family."

She leaned in and brushed a kiss across his lips. "Don't you know we already are?"

For the first time in forever, Callum felt truly at home. He knew in his heart that the joy of this moment would last forever.

Epilogue

"I like seeing you smile."

Becky turned toward Callum as he parked the truck in front of the Paws and Claws Animal Clinic, so much happiness filling her heart she could almost feel it beating against her rib cage. It was another Texas blue-sky day, the brightness of the sunshine reflecting the glow in her heart.

"You make me smile, Mr. Fortune," she told him.

"For the rest of our lives, Mrs. Fortune," he answered.

She glanced down at her left hand and the eternity band that had joined the engagement ring on her finger.

It had been a little less than a week since Callum proposed, and they'd driven to the county courthouse with the twins earlier that morning to exchange their wedding vows.

Some people might question a whirlwind courtship and wedding, but Becky didn't worry any longer about raising eyebrows. The moment Callum had sat down on the park bench with her, any doubts and fears she'd had fled like night shadows chased away by the light of dawn.

She'd felt her late husband's spirit surrounding them, a quiet whisper of approval that she could move forward and truly love again.

They were a family and had both wanted to make it official as soon as possible. With Callum's busy schedule, her dedication to the pediatric center and the continuing saga of baby Linus's future, a simple ceremony felt right.

Callum's stepmom got them to agree to celebrate with a larger reception once their lives calmed down a bit, although Becky wondered if that would ever happen. She didn't care. Becoming Callum's wife, even with no fanfare, fulfilled her in ways she couldn't have imagined.

They'd driven straight to the vet clinic so they could attend the afternoon's grand opening celebration and would begin the process of moving Becky and the girls to the ranch later that night.

As Becky opened the passenger door, Marci and David greeted her. Her new mother-in-law enveloped her in a tight hug, whispering words of congratulations into her ear.

"Welcome to the family," David told her when it was his turn for a hug.

"It makes me so happy to be a Fortune," she said, and the older man kissed both of her cheeks.

"I'm a grandma," Marci murmured as Callum put Luna into her arms.

"Gigi," the girl said with a toothy grin, staring into Marci's eyes.

"That's perfect," the older woman said, blinking back tears. "I'm your Gigi."

"And you can call me Papa." David held out his hands for Sasha, who automatically reached for him. Once again, the Fortune charm had worked its magic on Becky's cautious daughter.

"Papa," Sasha repeated.

"Uh-oh." Callum shut the door and placed an arm around Becky's shoulders, pulling her close. "I have a feeling our girls are going to be spoiled rotten by their Gigi and Papa."

"Nothing rotten about spoiling our granddaughters." Marci looked between Becky and Callum. "You've made us so very happy."

Becky nodded, unable to speak around the emotion clogging her throat. The sense of contentment she felt at being a part of the Fortune family almost overwhelmed her.

Callum squeezed her arm. "Let's go check out the new vet clinic. I'm sure the rest of the family will be champing at the bit to give you a proper welcome."

"It feels like they already have," Becky told him. The triplets had arrived yesterday and they'd had a big family dinner at the ranch. It amazed her how warm and gracious every member of Callum's family seemed to be. They made her feel as if she belonged with them, and she knew that whatever life brought, she could handle it surrounded by that depth of love.

As much as Becky loved Rambling Rose, she'd found

her true home with Callum. Gratitude bubbled up inside her along with an abiding joy. Tragedy had marked her but not defined the whole of who she was.

She linked her arm with her husband's as they headed toward the new building, thrilled to walk toward their future together.

* * * * *

We've got some exciting changes coming in our February 2020 Special Edition books!
Our covers have been redesigned, and the emotional contemporary romances from your favorite authors will be longer in length.

Be sure to come back next month for more great stories from Special Edition!

Look for the next installment of the new continuity The Fortunes of Texas: Rambling Rose

Don't miss
Fortune's Texas Surprise
by USA TODAY *bestselling author*
Stella Bagwell

On sale February 2020,
wherever Harlequin books and
ebooks are sold.

YOU HAVE
JUST READ A
HARLEQUIN®
SPECIAL
EDITION
BOOK.

Discover more heartfelt tales of **family, friendship** and **love** from the Harlequin Special Edition series. Be sure to look for all six Harlequin® Special Edition books every month.

#2743 FORTUNE'S TEXAS SURPRISE
The Fortunes of Texas: Rambling Rose • by Stella Bagwell
Until he meets foster mother Stephanie Fortune, rancher Acton Donovan has never pictured himself as a family man. Now suddenly he's thinking about wedding rings and baby cradles! But can he convince himself he's good enough for a woman from the prominent Fortune family?

#2744 FOR THE TWINS' SAKE
Dawson Family Ranch • by Melissa Senate
Bachelor cowboy Noah Dawson finds a newborn on his doorstep with a note that it's his baby, but the infant girl's surprise identity changes his life forever. Now he's reunited with Sara Mayhew, his recently widowed ex-girlfriend, and they're spending Christmas together for the twins' sake—at least, that's what they keep telling themselves...

#2745 A CHANCE FOR THE RANCHER
Match Made in Haven • by Brenda Harlen
Patrick Stafford trades his suit for a Stetson and risks it all on a dude ranch. But it's the local vet, Dr. Brooke Langley, who really challenges him. Is this playboy rancher ready to take a risk on a single mom and become a family man?

#2746 HER HOMECOMING WISH
Gallant Lake Stories • by Jo McNally
Being the proverbial good girl left her brokenhearted and alone. Now Mackenzie Wallace is back and wants excitement with her old crush. She hopes there's still some bad boy lurking beneath the single father's upright exterior. Dan Adams isn't the boy he was—but secrets from his past might still manage to keep them apart.

#2747 DAUGHTER ON HIS DOORSTEP
by Teresa Southwick
When Luke McCoy moved next door, Shelby Richards knew he'd discover the truth. Within minutes, young Emma was on his doorstep, asking Luke if he really was her daddy. Shelby had her reasons, but Luke is not so quick to forgive. And as Shelby saw Luke with their daughter, her heart was not so quick to forget what they'd all missed out on.

#2748 THE BARTENDER'S SECRET
Masterson, Texas • by Caro Carson
Quiet, sheltered, educated, shy Shakespeare professor Delphinia Ray is way out of Connor McClaine's league. So he tries to push her away, convinced she can't handle the harsh truth about his past. But maybe Delphinia is the one to help him face his demons...

Get 4 FREE REWARDS!

We'll send you 2 FREE Books plus <u>2 FREE Mystery Gifts</u>.

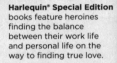

Harlequin® Special Edition books feature heroines finding the balance between their work life and personal life on the way to finding true love.

FREE
Value Over
$20

YES! Please send me 2 FREE Harlequin® Special Edition novels and my 2 FREE gifts (gifts are worth about $10 retail). After receiving them, if I don't wish to receive any more books, I can return the shipping statement marked "cancel." If I don't cancel, I will receive 6 brand-new novels every month and be billed just $4.99 per book in the U.S. or $5.74 per book in Canada. That's a savings of at least 12% off the cover price! It's quite a bargain! Shipping and handling is just 50¢ per book in the U.S. and $1.25 per book in Canada.* I understand that accepting the 2 free books and gifts places me under no obligation to buy anything. I can always return a shipment and cancel at any time. The free books and gifts are mine to keep no matter what I decide.

235/335 HDN GNMP

Name (please print)

Address   Apt. #

City   State/Province   Zip/Postal Code

Mail to the **Reader Service:**
IN U.S.A.: P.O. Box 1341, Buffalo, NY 14240-8531
IN CANADA: P.O. Box 603, Fort Erie, Ontario L2A 5X3

Want to try 2 free books from another series! Call 1-800-873-8635 or visit www.ReaderService.com.

Love Harlequin romance?

DISCOVER.

Be the first to find out about promotions, news and exclusive content!

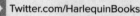 Facebook.com/HarlequinBooks

Twitter.com/HarlequinBooks

Instagram.com/HarlequinBooks

Pinterest.com/HarlequinBooks

ReaderService.com

EXPLORE.

Sign up for the Harlequin e-newsletter and download a free book from any series at **TryHarlequin.com**.

CONNECT.

Join our Harlequin community to share your thoughts and connect with other romance readers!
Facebook.com/groups/HarlequinConnection

 **HARLEQUIN**®

ROMANCE WHEN YOU NEED IT